Unmated

Devilish #6

Charity Parkerson

Punk & Sissy Publications

Copyright

Punk
&
Sissy

—Warning: This book is intended for readers over the age of 18. Some of my books contain allusions to past abuse and trauma.

Editor: BZ Hercules & Consultants

Cover art: Charity Parkerson

Contents

Introduction

Aspen and Leif spent more than fifty years together with no hope of being true mates. Things are shaking up in the world of fated mates. Now, it may be too late.

After falling in love with Leif decades ago, Aspen's pack rejected him. Bears aren't supposed to waste time on vampires. Even without hope of a true mating, Aspen loved Leif deeply. Still does, even though he was the one who ended things. Now Weres are being paired with vampire and Aspen can't see himself with anyone else. Unfortunately, Leif hates him now. That's something he doesn't know how to overcome.

Leif thought he had gotten to a point where he could survive since losing Aspen. Now Aspen's back, and so too are the feelings he packed away. He doesn't know if he can risk his heart again. Just because the rules have changed doesn't mean they'll be paired. While Leif is torn between running and staying, the community he swore to protect is falling to shambles. If Frost pays the price for Leif's indecision, Celeste will see them all dead. It's time to pick a lane.

Unmated is the sixth book in Charity Parkerson's series where vampires, Weres, demons, gods, and all manner of the supernatural live together beneath the noses of humankind. These books are best when read in order.

Chapter One

There was something bittersweet about unpacking boxes in a new home alone. When Aspen had walked away from everything in Montana to come to Wulfe, Washington, chasing his ex, he never thought the change would be permanent. In fact, when Leif had thoroughly rejected him, Aspen had thought to get in his old beat-up pickup and keep driving until he ran out of money or his tires fell off. But finding a friend in Wulfe had him feeling a way he hadn't in a long time, like he had family again. Of course, a big casino win had also opened all the doors for him. Leif disappeared—again—and Aspen gave up. Some bears weren't meant to find love. It seemed Aspen was on that list. So he took his newfound riches and settled for the only thing that comforted him at all—being near Kyrie. Kyrie was a young wolf mated to an ancient vampire. That friendship would be enough. Having a large bank account ensured he could live wherever he wanted now.

At the end of the day, he had to live somewhere. He knew he could stay in bear form and enjoy thriving in nature for the rest of his days. But Aspen didn't want to be lonely anymore, and he preferred life as a man. He had already met a few of his neighbors. Aspen would stay here... even though Leif had moved on. It was time to let go of that dream.

When he had broken things off to spare them a much bigger pain down the line, Aspen had made the biggest mistake of his life. He had tried talking to Leif, working things out, but Leif just ran. They were over. Aspen had to live with that now.

As Aspen pulled items from the box he unpacked, something fell to the floor. Aspen picked it up. It was a photo of Leif and him. Logically, Aspen knew they never aged, but it felt odd for the image to look like it had been taken yesterday. He couldn't stop staring. They looked so happy. Aspen couldn't even remember what happiness felt like. He lovingly stroked Leif's face, forever frozen in time. Damn. Time was supposed to heal all wounds. That was bullshit. Being without Leif hadn't even gotten easier to carry, much less heal. He had done this to himself. That knowledge didn't ease the pain. In fact, the situation being his fault made things worse. Leif wouldn't let him take it back. Now here he was: trapped in stasis.

The doorbell rang, yanking Aspen from a growing depression. He tossed the picture into the trash before moving to answer the door. The northwest's pack leader, Waylon, stood on his doorstep. Waylon was always all smiles when Aspen saw him. Aspen liked him. Just another reason to stay.

"We've come to help."

For a moment, the claim confused Aspen. Waylon's six-foot-five frame blocked the doorway. "We?" Even as he asked the question Aspen stepped aside, inviting Waylon inside.

The moment Waylon moved, he revealed a slightly shorter man with light brown skin. His eyes were a very unique green. They were almost two colors, with a vivid green slowly going to light blue around his pupils. They were mesmerizing.

Waylon motioned behind him. "Yeah. This is Lysander. He was free and eager to help a neighbor and—hopefully—potential pack member."

That statement had Aspen tearing his gaze away from Lysander's eyes. He knew he had to look every bit as shocked as he was. "What?"

Waylon's smile somehow got brighter. "Yeah. You live here now. We'd love for you to join us."

Aspen didn't know how to react.

Lysander saved him. "It's nice to meet you."

A nervous chuckle escaped Aspen as he accepted Lysander's outstretched hand to shake. "You too."

Waylon motioned toward the door. "Would you like some help carrying in furniture? We can work together to make it look hard." Waylon's offer was filled with laughter. Humans lived in Wulfe too, so they had to hide their strength sometimes.

"That's why everything is still in the truck. I hadn't figured out how to bring everything in alone without raising some eyebrows. Since I've only met the wolves on either side of me, I don't know if I have any human neighbors."

Waylon motioned toward the front door again. "Yeah. The houses across the street, two and three doors down, are human."

Lysander cut in. "My cousin lives directly across from you. They're on vacation right now, but they asked me to tell you they can't wait to meet you when they get back."

That was nice. When Aspen had chosen Leif all those decades ago, his pack had rejected him. Even the ones who were blood didn't want anything to do with a bear who lowered himself to date a vampire. He had always known his family had their prejudices. It hadn't surprised Aspen at all when they walked away. He was pretty certain they had been waiting for an excuse.

"I'm excited to meet them, and I'm grateful for the help. It's not like I own a ton of stuff, but everything has still been overwhelming. Of course, it's kind of my fault for choosing to do all this while Kyrie and Fen are on their honeymoon."

Waylon squeezed his shoulder. "Well, you have a huge pack here. We take care of each other. Let's unload that truck."

The offer warmed his chest. He felt truly welcome for the first time, and he couldn't cry and look like a baby. Pack was extremely important to Weres. It had been a nightmare being a lone bear.

Most Weres were social creatures who put a lot of stock in their family. He saw people with their nonstop get-togethers and holiday celebrations. Aspen didn't have that. He had felt isolated as hell for a long time. Whatever he needed to do to join Waylon's pack, he was in.

Aspen led the way, and the three of them had everything inside in no time. They chatted and laughed. It was a good day. When the sun dipped low, Waylon left to be with his vampire husband. Aspen had to admit he had forgotten that part of Waylon's life for a moment. The heartache and jealousy were real, but pointless. Aspen was moving on. Yep, that was what he was doing.

Lysander stayed to help Aspen unpack. They worked side by side in the kitchen in silence. It wasn't uncomfortable. In fact, they worked well together, seeming to easily dodge each other as if they choreographed their steps. There was one thing killing him, and Aspen couldn't take it any longer.

"You smell like magic." Aspen didn't look Lysander's way or ask questions. He simply opened the door to getting to know Lysander better. Lysander could choose to leave the statement hanging there.

Lysander laughed. It was a musical sound that made every hair on Aspen's body—which was a lot—stand on end. "I'm a fairy."

Okay, Aspen had all the plans to be nosy now. He wanted all the details. "Seriously? That's cool. I don't think I've ever met a fairy before."

"You've seen us. You just didn't know you were seeing us."

That was kind of an odd thing to say. Aspen didn't know how to respond. He was pretty dang certain he hadn't seen one before, but what did he know? It was not like he had recognized Lysander as a fairy. Maybe he had seen one before. Aspen did his best to keep the conversation rolling. "Are there many fairies in Wulfe?"

"Yes, and no."

Aspen had no idea what that meant.

Thankfully, Lysander didn't keep him guessing. "Most of us live in Faerie. It's kind of an invisible place inside of another place. My home is here in Wulfe. You just can't see it."

None of Lysander's claims made sense to him, but he was just a bear. He didn't know much about anything. "That sounds cool. It's a shame I can't see it. I bet it's magical as hell, judging by how powerful the scent of your magic is."

Lysander let out a loud guffaw that had Aspen smiling. "Did you just say I stink?"

Aspen blushed. "No. I think you smell very nice." His blush deepened by the second.

Lysander's smile never dimmed. "I'll cook for you sometime. Then you can go to Faerie."

Aspen hadn't grinned this much for real in a while. It felt nice to do so now. "I'd love that."

They shared a smile and went back to unpacking, except the silence disappeared. They chatted about anything and everything for hours. It was a good night.

Leif didn't know whether to be thankful for the fairy for masking Leif's scent with his overwhelming magic. He kind of wanted to rip the fucker's throat out. If he could. Aspen was right. Lysander smelled like some of the most powerful magic Leif had come across in years. It wasn't exactly more than his king or even Frost, the town's healer. He smelled different. Being born druid made it easy for Leif to recognize magic, but this was the type of thing he imagined even humans caught a whiff of as they passed. That was unfortunate. Fairies were sexual beings. It wasn't exactly their food source. Drawing orgasms from others was a draining of energy. A powerful energy. Making someone come was like dessert for them, and they were a gluttonous species.

While cloaking his presence, Leif listened to every word of their conversations. They were well suited to be friends. Of course, Aspen was built for friendship. His sweet demeanor and cuddly-bear charm drew people to him like honey enchanted Aspen. He was too nice for this world, and he had to live in it for eternity. At one time, Leif had enjoyed every second of protecting that purity. That had been the job Leif wanted most in the world.

Lysander pulled another loud laugh from Aspen. Leif returned to thinking about tearing out his throat. He had no idea why he was like this, stalking a life he could have if he only reached for it. His anger and hurt were too thick.

“Enjoying the view?”

Celeste appeared. No one reacted, so Leif assumed he was the only one blinded by heaven's light. She was beautiful, likely the most beautiful thing in creation. Leif couldn't look away.

Celeste circled him as if inspecting him. "Are you entertained watching that first spark? All I have to do is snap my fingers, and this night will be an inferno. Aspen would never think of you again." Each word hit its mark. After Aspen came to town, Leif deserted his post guarding Frost. That position had been assigned to him by Celeste. He currently disobeyed her wishes. She could snap her fingers and turn him to dust. Maybe she would.

A musical laugh cut through the air. "That's not a fitting punishment. Death is the easy way out."

Oh, she was for real pissed. "Why should I continue sacrificing my time for a goddess who sees me suffer and does nothing? It's not like Frost can't take care of himself." Leif knew spewing his anger was a bad decision, but she likely wouldn't destroy him. She had been having too much fun watching him suffer for the last two years. A point reiterated now that he saw her again. She might have been disguised at the time, but her eyes never changed. She had played waitress at the casino one night, getting an up-close view of the lives she destroyed. He might as well get to say why he left her service, since she liked playing games. Honestly, he hoped she lost her temper and ended his suffering. It was overdue.

Celeste stopped pacing. "Do you think I don't fret over every mate pairing? I suppose you think being a god is easy and truly all fun and games. Of course, you do. Look at you staring at what you can still have while too scared to reach for him. Maybe he deserves the fairy. He gave up everything for you. Weres deeply love their packs, no matter how terrible that family is. They abandoned him because he chose you." Celeste turned and eyed Aspen. Pride and love etched her features. "He truly is a testament to Odin. My love knows how to make them." Celeste focused on Leif again. "Frost is my nephew."

Oh, fuck. He had not known that when abandoning his post.

"He's now missing."

God fucking damnit. She really would pair Aspen with Lysander. If he ever had any chance of becoming Aspen's true mate, he had destroyed it.

"You have exactly to the minute two weeks to prove to me you deserve to be Aspen's mate."

"He broke things off with me."

Celeste simply held his stare, giving Leif time to accept a lot of harsh truths about himself. She didn't even need to list them. Just staring into her eyes showed him his unadulterated self.

"Two weeks or he's Lysander's. Use your time wisely."

"What about Frost?"

Her stare cut through him, and then she was gone. Sound rushed back to him like the TV had been on mute.

"Yeah. I mean, I just put away the cookware, so I already know where everything is."

Aspen's bright smile hadn't dampened. "I'm intrigued. Just tell me what you need."

While holding Aspen's stare, Lysander's arm swept over the stove. Steam rolled from pots that magically appeared. A delicious scent filled the air. "I've got you."

The way Aspen bit his bottom lip, visibly trying to fight the smile that hadn't budged, said everything. His two weeks had begun. After Lysander fed Aspen, he could pull Aspen into Faerie and out of Leif's reach forever. No sooner than that depressing thought hit, Aspen turned toward the stove and Lysander focused on Leif—like he had known he was there the entire time. Lysander smirked, and Leif's heart sank. It was possible he had already lost, even before the battle had begun.

Chapter Two

ASPEN TRAILED THROUGH THE aisles at the grocery store, stuck in a weird head-space. He had honestly had a fantastic night with Lysander. For some reason, he felt off about the situation. Lysander had said and done all the right things. Aspen couldn't wait to see him again. But there was something gnawing at his gut, and he already knew it was Leif. Leif existed somewhere in the world. Aspen would move on if it killed him. It was just... Leif existed somewhere out there in the world. He hated the way this love twisted him and destroyed him. He would not waste his life on the past. Aspen would have a new pack. He could start over and not choose Leif. Aspen had to move on. If not, loving Leif might really kill him.

That thought solidified his decision to never look back. His nose hit the air. Tears blurred his vision. He immediately turned toward the meat selection nearby. Aspen would not acknowledge Leif's presence in the store. The scent got stronger. Fuck! He thought Leif had decided to leave this town, so Aspen thought he would be safe to stay. If Leif was here and they constantly crossed paths, Aspen needed to grow a backbone. The scent got stronger.

Aspen's stomach muscles tightened. He fought to keep his eyes open when he wanted to cut off every other sense so he could savor the smell of Leif.

“Hey.”

The softly spoken greeting weakened Aspen’s knees. There was no stopping his head from turning. As always, the first sight of Leif’s light blue eyes seared into his soul. Fuck. The love just never stopped, and it was genuinely pulling him toward the grave.

Aspen swallowed past the lump in his throat. “Hey. I thought you'd left town.”

Leif rubbed the back of his neck and shifted from foot to foot. “Yeah. It turns out I’m not as capable of walking away from everything as I thought. Audor is here.”

Aspen nodded. He should have known Leif wouldn't truly abandon his best friend. At his core, Leif was a soldier—loyal 'til the end. Aspen took a deep breath. "If I had known you planned to come back, I wouldn't have settled here. I know you don't want me around." Aspen averted his eyes at the last second. He couldn't watch Leif's growing disappointment in having to cross paths with Aspen.

"You're good. They have a unique pack here. Very accepting. You can have the support system you've always wanted. It's cruel to expect such a cuddly bear to miss his chance at having an actual family."

He couldn't breathe. Aspen had to get out of here.

"Hey. It's Aspen, right?"

Aspen turned toward the chipper female voice. A tiny, brown-haired woman waited for his attention.

"That's me."

Her smile brightened. The unique light of an animal flashed in her eyes. He smelled wolf.

She held out her hand. "I'm Vixen. Waylon sent me your way."

Aspen shook her hand while acutely aware of Leif's presence.

Vixen focused on Leif for half a second. "Hey, Leif."

"Hi."

Leif didn't sound annoyed. He didn't sound any certain way at all. Aspen was an inner wreck trying to figure out why Leif was still standing there.

Vixen's gaze locked on him again. "Waylon said you were a handyman back in Montana."

Aspen nodded, hoping he didn't look as nervous as he felt. Not only was Aspen pretty shy, Leif had shifted closer to him.

Vixen kept talking, seemingly oblivious to his inner struggle. "My fridge bit the dust. I have a newborn at home and a desperate need to keep things from spoiling. The wol—" Vixen caught herself. "The guy who usually does that sort of thing for us is slammed with work. Everyone's heat and air units are failing like crazy because of the unusually hot weather. He can't help me until next week. My husband owns a landscaping business. He'd be more than happy to—"

"I'll fix it," Aspen said, cutting her off. "Just let me know the address and I'll head that way as soon as I finish here." She had a newborn, and that was rare for Weres. For some odd reason, Wulfe seemed to have a higher birth survival rate than anywhere he had seen before.

It's Frost. He's the reason so many Weres are moving here. His success rate in keeping various species and their offspring alive through childbirth is abnormally high.

Aspen tried to ignore the words Leif forced into his head. As a druid, Leif could do that, and the memories of Leif in his head were choking him.

Vixen wore a huge grin. “Seriously? That’s so amazing. I can’t thank you enough.”

“That’s what we do. Help each other.” He didn’t want to use the word “pack” in a store where any human could overhear.

She happy-clapped while bouncing on her toes before settling down again. “I’m the coral-colored house on Oak Street. You can’t miss it.”

The first kernel of hope grew inside Aspen. If Vixen was any indication, it seemed like the town might really accept him into their pack. Pack life was a lot like skill-sharing communities. Everyone pitched in to help one another, and the pack thrived.

Vixen waved, saying her goodbyes to him and Leif.

The nervousness returned the moment they were alone again. His gaze slid back to Leif. He was still there and just as sexy as ever. Goddamn. A real Viking was hard as hell to resist. Leif had the whole hardened body with long blond hair shaved to the scalp on both sides, making his hair like a Mohawk that fell to the center of his back. Today, Leif had it tied back, but Aspen had felt that silky smooth hair slip over his skin as Leif kissed his way down Aspen's body. Damn. Seeing him really hurt.

Aspen motioned to his cart. "Well, I guess I need to finish this up so I can get that fridge running. It was nice seeing you."

Aspen pushed his cart a step farther.

Leif stepped backwards, staying with him. "See me again tonight."

The demand was a knife to the center of Aspen's chest. "I actually have a date tonight." Aspen nearly choked on the words, but Leif needed to know.

Leif didn't flinch or back down. "Then see me tomorrow night."

Leif looked hopeful.

Aspen felt sick. "I know it's my fault." The words came out sounding quiet. He couldn't make his voice go any louder. Too many emotions were stuck in his throat. "But you've already made it abundantly clear you don't want me. You don't want us. I have to move on before this ends me—like for real. Like *dead,* dead."

"Just see me. I swear you won't get hurt in any way."

"You can't swear that." Aspen didn't know if Leif had intended to say more, but he had to stop things there. If they got back together, they still might not be true mates. They still might get hurt. Aspen had been more than willing to take that chance when he came to town, but Leif's rejection had cut him to the bone. Aspen would freely admit he deserved that rebuff. However, he had to stop setting himself on fire in the name of hope.

Leif grabbed Aspen's shopping cart so he couldn't get away. "I won't let you get hurt."

Aspen drew a slow breath in through his nose. "Can I think about it?"

He felt Leif poking around inside his brain, searching for any lie in Aspen's request. Aspen knew Leif well enough to know he wouldn't let Aspen walk away until he was satisfied Aspen truly intended to do just as he claimed he would.

Leif let go of the cart. "Just let me know."

With a sharp nod, Aspen walked away and wrapped himself in his broken heart. He would think about seeing Leif again. Odin knew that was all Aspen could think about now. But for real, he didn't think he could survive losing Leif again. He had ripped out his own soul when he ended things. Aspen desperately wanted that missing piece back. Unfortunately, he was pretty sure that living without that piece of himself had already killed him.

As much as Leif desperately wanted to hide and follow Aspen around all day, he needed to figure out where Frost was. As he had told Aspen, Frost was the reason this town's population was growing. Without him, a lot of pregnant Weres were in danger, and they would turn on Frost in a second once all these women started dying. That was a battle even the nephew of Celeste didn't want.

While Leif had been too angry last night to truly hear Celeste out, he had heard her. Every word she said just didn't sink in until later, and she had said a lot. As far as Leif knew, Celeste had only one sibling: Lucifer. How was it even possible that Lucifer had spawned a child, and no one knew? It had to have been a cataclysmic event. Frost wasn't that old. He didn't understand.

Next, was being Lucifer's child the reason Frost could hide from someone as powerful as Celeste? Seriously, why couldn't she find him? It was possible Frost was in terrible danger. Leif knew nothing about the circumstances of his disappearance. He felt woefully unprepared to even know where to start.

Additionally, Celeste had called Odin her love. Was that how and why Weres were suddenly capable of having vampire mates? Everything about this entire situation, from the first day he had been sent to Wulfe until now, was nothing short of baffling.

Leif knew the best place to start was with Audor. Audor and he had been best friends for as far back as he could recall. Since Leif had skipped out with only a note left behind, he didn't know how Audor would react to seeing him again.

As he strolled out of the grocery store and into the street, he caught sight of something that stumped him beyond words. Wulfe was very much one of those small towns where the diner and grocery store were on Main Street alongside the freshly kept lawns of medium-income homes. Everyone knew everyone, and most places were within walking distance if a person lived on one of the many streets in what was considered "town." People who lived in or around the forest were a different matter. But when the weather was nice, it wasn't uncommon to see people milling around outside, doing yard work or walking and jogging. That was why it shouldn't have caught his eye to see a lone man walking from home to home, except it was Frost.

Leif jogged across the street. "Frost!"

Frost froze and turned his way, looking confused. "You can see me?"

Leif's forehead furrowed. "Of course I can see you. I thought you were missing and had everyone looking for you, most especially Celeste."

"No. Seriously. How can you see me?"

It hit Leif. Frost was cloaked in magic. Strong druid magic wiped his existence from the map, making him impossible to find... unless someone had druid blood—like Leif.

"Oh." He didn't know why the realization shocked him so much. He had known—as a healer—Frost would possess powerful abilities. Leif just hadn't known Frost knew how to use them.

Frost looked slightly panicked. His gaze shot around, openly searching for the edges of his spellwork.

Leif rushed to reassure him. “You’re safe. I have druid blood as well. Plus, you have wards up only meant to hide from everything else in existence. You have to add a separate ward to be invisible to me.”

“Oh.” Frost didn’t look relieved. “I didn’t know that. So...” He tapped his foot, looking nervous.

Even though Leif didn’t know why Frost hid, he completely understood the desire to disappear. “Don’t worry. I won’t tell anyone where you are. But could you at least tell me what’s going on? I leave town for a few weeks and the whole world turns on its head.”

Frost cleared his throat. "I'm guessing anyone looking your way right now thinks you're talking to yourself."

A smile exploded across Leif's face. "I suppose they do."

Frost visibly relaxed a hair. "Sorry. You're right. A lot has happened since you left. I need to stay hidden for my mental health. At least for a little while. I can't abandon my patients, though."

Leif eyed Frost's wards. He had them secured to where only a certain list of people could see him. Leif couldn't read the names. Those were hidden, but Leif's curiosity rose by the second. "It's that bad, huh?"

A wry-sounding laugh burst from Frost. "I'm not even sure." He waved a hand toward the wards that would be invisible to anyone else. "For now, this is my life while I make some big decisions. I just need some time, and no one will let me have it. So, Gemini taught me this."

Leif's eyebrows rose. "Gemini?"

Frost nodded. "His mom is pretty close with a druid priestess. He knows a trick or two. We also visited his mom to get more tips."

"Leif."

At the sound of his name, Leif turned his head. He found Gemini on the side-walk surrounded by the same faint circle of symbols. What the fuck was actually happening?

When their gazes met, Gemini shook his head and moved closer. "Damn. You really can see us." Gemini shared a look with Frost. He imagined they held a private conversation, like mates tended to do. Gemini focused on him again. "Let's go for a walk and let Frost work."

Leif cast a quick glance around to ensure no one was watching. With a single gesture, a matching dome surrounded him, hiding him from all eyes. He didn't go as far as Frost and Gemini. There was no need to create a list of names or anything like that. Leif only hoped Celeste didn't check in on him and find him missing too. But he also didn't relish looking too crazy while Gemini and he talked.

Frost went to the door of his next patient, and Leif moved to the sidewalk with Gemini. Gemini stayed quiet for a few minutes.

Leif allowed the silence to grow. He wasn't uncomfortable. Leif had gone decades over the centuries without speaking to another living soul besides Audor. They had known each other for way too long to have many conversations left in them.

"Frost says you haven't heard the news. I'm torn on what to say because you will find out sooner or later."

Leif nodded. "Talk travels fast in a small community."

Gemini stopped and met Leif's stare. "Here's the thing. You can obviously see us, and what I have to say might make you feel differently about Frost. But my mate deserves peace, and this community needs him. If your knowing we're still here puts Frost in any danger whatsoever, we'll be forced to create stronger barriers elsewhere. I'm sick of seeing our world do its best to tear him to pieces. All he does is give, and all everyone else does is take. But I will take him from here, and we'll spend eternity in our own bubble before I let our kind destroy him. Fuck this town."

Leif nodded along. Every word Gemini said only served to confuse him even more. "Okay. If you haven't noticed, I'm not in a real good place with our world either. Walking away from my post meant turning my back on Celeste. I imagine my punishment will come at any time now." He knew what that price would be, but Gemini didn't need to know any of that.

Gemini took a deep breath. "Celeste wasn't quite honest about why she wanted Frost so protected."

It hit Leif. He knew exactly where this was headed. "Oh. Is this about Frost being Lucifer's son?"

Gemini's eyebrows shot up. "Wow. You said that so casually, as if that wasn't enough to make him a pariah among immortals."

Leif shrugged. "Obviously, Lucifer ripped Audor's leg off when we annoyed him, but—honestly—I feel safer knowing Frost is his son. Not only does that explain the weird soft spot Lucifer has always had for him, but I doubt he'll destroy the place where his son lives. Frost's existence might be the thing sparing the world right now."

"In my mom's opinion, she thinks Lucifer doesn't know."

Leif shook his head. "How could he not know? He's a god."

"For the same reason Celeste can't see him now. Magic. A druid priestess my mom knows says someone pulled some powerful spell work to hide Frost. Whether it was his great aunt—since his powers showed up after her passing—or someone she knew, the druid involved had to be imposing. Even the priestess couldn't deconstruct it. Since we're dealing with Lucifer, it was her opinion false memories were created of his true parentage to keep him safe."

"Why would she let him stay in the dark about something so important? His life could be at stake. Every tainted creature alive will hunt him."

Gemini shrugged. "Maybe she thought his not knowing was enough to protect him when she passed. All of this is purely speculation. With everyone we could ask gone, except Lucifer, we can't know how he came to be or if Lucifer even knows. All we know is this is a lot, and I'm done allowing free access to my mate for everyone's use and abuse. He's taking care of the pregnant Weres in this town, doing his best to make sure as many survive as possible. Otherwise, the closed for business sign is out. I've sat back too long and watched him killing himself for everyone else."

Leif didn't even have to think about it. If anyone stressed Aspen the way everyone had stressed Frost, expecting him to be a twenty-four-hour miracle worker, Leif would have snapped a hell of a lot sooner. "You don't have to worry. I won't say anything. You'd be surprised how much I can hide. No one beyond Audor and now Frost and you know I was born druid." Leif chuckled. "And I use my magic all the time." His hands lifted and fell. "No one really sees me. It's always been that way. An invisible foot soldier and nothing else." He hadn't meant to get so personal and let his bitterness spill out, but fuck. A life of service with zero reward was enough to break anyone. "Good for you for protecting your mate."

Gemini squeezed his shoulder. "Thank you. Using his skills to help others is important to Frost. But sometimes you have to know when to walk away. Sometimes it takes someone else to decide for you."

Gemini's words took his breath. He was right. The fear of losing Aspen had Leif sick all hours of the night and day when they were together. Every day, it had gotten worse, until he turned into someone else. Aspen had loved him enough to set him free. Now they had a real shot, and Leif had pissed on all Aspen's sacrifices. Leif had no idea how to fix it.

With his heart in his throat, Frost left his last patient's house. Gemini waited for him—alone—on the sidewalk. His mate's thoughts were soothing and sweet. He was proud of Frost, and his love consumed Frost every second of the day. There were no thoughts of being found or worries of being exposed. That let Frost breathe easier. Then Gemini smiled, and Frost nearly missed a step. He was so pretty. Every day, he got sexier to Frost, and that seemed almost impossible since he kept Frost mesmerized.

Frost wanted to run his fingers through his long, soft locks. Goddess, he was just everything to Frost.

Gemini's expression turned loving. "Same, baby."

As much as Frost knew Gemini was in his head every second of the day, he still hadn't gotten used to someone hearing every thought he had.

Frost kept moving until they were nearly toe to toe. "Done. Everyone is doing fine."

Gemini took his hand. "Ready to go home?"

"We should stop by the house and check on it. I don't want anyone thinking they can just move in and take over or whatever."

Gemini nodded along. "Sounds great."

Frost took a shaky breath. Even though he had been using his magic for a bit, he still hadn't gotten comfortable moving through space and time to get anywhere with a single thought. His biggest fear was losing Gemini somewhere along the way. "I guess this is it."

Gemini held his stare like the rock he was. "You couldn't lose me even if you tried. I believe in you."

With a sharp nod, Frost braced his feet and held tightly to Gemini's hand. He envisioned their cabin, and they were there. Frost took a breath. They were okay. Together, they moved around the cabin, checking each room. Everything looked the same until they reached his home clinic. His entire desk and the surrounding floor were covered in stacks of books.

"What in the hell?" Frost moved to the first pile. Before he inspected the top book, he spotted a note on a stack nearby. Frost leaned closer to read it. For some reason, he didn't want to touch anything. He read the note aloud. "Frost, these are the books on medical care for each species and cross-species that you've been wanting. I'm sorry I didn't tell you sooner that you're my nephew. When I lured you to Wulfe, I only knew you were a powerful druid with awakening powers. It wasn't until you called out for Lucifer, and he came to you, that I realized there had to be more to you. Lucifer would never come for a single damn soul crying out in distress. His bitterness and anger mean too much to him. I knew I had to look deeper. You come from a powerful line. It took a lot of research and hunting to find the truth, but you're his. I didn't know what to say. The last thing I wanted was to feel as if I had failed you the way I failed Tam.

Please know that you are loved and wanted. I know you've needed these books for research. If you decide to come home, I'll wait for you to come to me. You're owed the choice. Love, Auntie Celeste."

Frost turned Gemini's way.

Gemini looked resigned, as if he already knew what Frost would choose. He chose Gemini.

"Are you ready to go? It looks like everything here is fine."

Gemini's eyebrows rose. "I feel how badly you want to be here to help the community."

Frost closed the distance between them. "Then I know you also feel the way you're more important to me. Let's go back to Tibet. I can't go back to you feeling stuck in last place. You are and will always be my first choice."

Gemini flashed him a wry smile. "You know that's not entirely true. I know I'm your first everything, but *you* felt like I was stuck last because of the way you've been torn in a million directions. Whatever makes you the happiest is what I'll do."

Frost held Gemini's stare. "You make me the happiest."

Gemini rubbed Frost's arms, as if trying to warm him. "How about this? We stay hidden for a little while longer, but we do it here. You can relax, read your books, and still be within shouting distance if a true emergency arises. I get to rub your feet and kiss any place I want on this delectable body." He shuffled closer, tempting Frost in every way. "When you're ready, we'll wipe away the wards."

"Kiss anywhere you want, huh?"

"Yep," Gemini said, making the *p* pop.

Frost couldn't stop smiling. "I've missed our bed."

Gemini grabbed two handfuls of Frost's ass and lifted. "Then let me reintroduce you to it."

Frost wrapped his legs around Gemini and buried his face against Gemini's neck. Everything felt easier when he let Gemini take control. Frost might not have any real answers yet, but he knew one thing. Gemini would always be there to look out for Frost no matter whose toes he smashed—even the Goddess herself.

Chapter Three

ASPEN COULDN'T RECALL THE last time he had been this nervous. It was ridiculous, considering he had just had dinner with Lysander the night before. He worried too much over his clothes. Aspen was a bear. What the fuck did he know about being stylish? Finally, he settled on a t-shirt that looked okay with his eyes, and comfortable jeans. He felt so off kilter, going on a date at his age. Aspen was an old bear. He wanted to chill and snack.

Before Aspen walked away from getting ready, he caught sight of his reflection and froze. There were dark circles under his eyes. Maybe he should just focus on becoming one with the pack. It had been a nice day, being useful and hearing all the pack gossip. He should stop dealing in matters of the heart. Aspen needed to turn to love for his community and away from romantic love. Just bury that shit.

Someone knocked on the door.

Aspen headed to answer. For a moment, he thought Lysander was early, but the scent of vampire hit him. It wasn't Leif. That was one scent he would never forget. Aspen opened the door to a vampire he had seen before but didn't know. It was one of the Scottish bunch sent to Wulfe to guard Frost.

"Yeah?" He knew he sounded rude and unwelcoming, which totally went against his nature. But there was a reason Aspen had steered clear of this one. There was something dark in him.

"Oh, good. I see we'll get along beautifully." There was a flirtatious yet sarcastic edge to his unexpected visitor.

Aspen didn't feel better.

"Why are you here?"

Aspen's brow furrowed. He had no idea what was happening. "Um. I live here. Why are you here?"

Blue eyes that looked unnatural with his strawberry blond hair rolled at his response. "I meant in Wulfe. Rumor is you've moved here and joined the local pack. Are you trying to break up the band? Leif has already disappeared because of you. You honestly have a lot of nerve deciding to stay."

Aspen's confusion couldn't have gotten deeper if it tried. "What?"

"You're Leif's ex. He ran away. Frost ended up missing with fewer guards to cover him. Does any of this ring a bell?"

"Stone?"

Lysander appeared behind the vamp, who was apparently named Stone. He held a bouquet of flowers that had a slight preternatural glow to them. Aspen's heart melted a hair. He loved flowers. Unfortunately, everything else happening got more confusing by the second.

"What are you doing here?"

Aspen thought it was odd for Lysander to question Stone's presence. It wasn't as if Lysander knew enough about Aspen's life to know who should or shouldn't be there, but really.

"I'd like to know the answer too."

Stone's expression underwent major renovations. The spiteful, accusatory edge disappeared. Stone turned into that guy everyone liked. "Lysander. Hey. It's always nice running into you." Each word dripped with sexual innuendo.

Lysander did not look pleased. "Wait." The flowers were unceremoniously shoved Aspen's way. He took them out of sheer bewilderment while Lysander went toe to toe with Stone. "Is this another one of your playmates? Everyone is just another bed to you."

"Absolutely not," Aspen said at the same time Stone threw out his denials. "No. It's not that."

Lysander rolled his eyes. "Don't give me that BS. It's no secret you've fucked everyone in this town."

"Not everyone." Stone's grumble sounded exactly like a kid's rebuttal after getting called to the carpet.

"What the hell is going on here?" Leif shoved his way through the fighting pair to stand at Aspen's side.

Aspen stared at Leif, wondering what the hell he was doing there. Aspen hated drama. Everything about this situation had him switching from one foot to the other, ready to hide. His breathing got faster by the second. Everyone spoke over everyone else.

Lysander shot him a look Aspen never expected to see. It looked a lot like hate. “Are you fucking everybody too?”

Aspen took a step back and shut the door. He turned the lock and slid the chain in place for good measure. While Aspen knew every creature on his front porch could simply swipe the door aside like it was made of toilet paper, he withdrew himself from whatever happened outside. Not his pig. Not his farm. Aspen was out. He had known rejoining the world of dating was a mistake. His fears were officially substantiated.

Aspen tuned out the noise and headed for the kitchen. He tossed the flowers in the trash and moved to the fridge. As he grabbed the handle, intent on getting a beer, he froze as he caught sight of a picture on the door that was held in place with a heart-shaped magnet. It was the picture of Leif and him he had thrown away yesterday. Aspen couldn't move. The panic attack he had feared tried to resurface. Why had he moved here? What was the point of anything at all? There was no happiness. Peace wasn't real. He was just a bear. Aspen should stick to that. He should leave everything behind and disappear. There was nothing for him anywhere.

Strong arms encircled him. Warm lips skimmed the shell of his ear. "Take a breath, cuddly bear." The soft words had Aspen sucking in a breath that sounded like a dying moose. He hadn't realized how close he had been to melting down.

Leif held him tighter, hugging Aspen to his chest. "Everything will be okay."

Aspen leaned forward and braced his forehead against the refrigerator, trying to center himself. The first tear fell. Another gasping breath brought with it the reality of him not escaping this breakdown. It had been long overdue.

"All I've ever wanted is for you to be happy. Every move I make is just another failure." He took another hard-fought breath. "I can't make any more decisions. It's too hard."

Aspen was a huge guy, but ancient vampire strength was bigger than most everything. While he fell apart, Leif carried him to bed. As they passed the front door, Leif touched the door. Wards glowed bright orange before vanishing. All outdoor sounds disappeared. Aspen felt the instant security. No one could break through the bubble Leif created for them. Aspen held tight to Leif and forced his mind blank. He hadn't been exaggerating. Aspen couldn't keep fighting this battle. Every decision he made only made things worse. He was done. Maybe he was finished with everything.

"Your thoughts hurt my chest." Leif climbed onto the bed and positioned their bodies where he could cuddle Aspen. A blanket flew upward and tucked them in.

Despite everything, a slight smile tugged at Aspen's lips. He had always loved it when Leif flexed his powers. He was majestic. Beautiful in his control of things unseen. He had always been out of Aspen's league. That was another lie he hadn't told. All Aspen wanted was Leif's happiness. It was killing him.

"Let me carry it."

A stuttered breath escaped Aspen at Leif's words. Leif was the strong one. Always had been. Aspen was the mess who couldn't handle a single shout.

Leif snuggled closer and kissed Aspen's forehead. "Your old pack was loud. Angry. Always wanting to hunt and kill. You've always been too good for them. I guess that's why I didn't realize how huge your sacrifice was by choosing me.

There was never a single day that I wanted anything other than a soft life with you. Sometimes that meant being abrasive to everyone else to protect you. But if I stole a life from you, I'm sorry for that. I didn't know choosing me cost so much."

No matter how upset and hurt he was, Aspen only regretted a single moment he spent with Leif. The moment he set Leif free.

Leif rubbed his back, soothing him. "Let it go. It's not like I've forgotten the constant fear of waking up one day to find you in love with some dumb bear who couldn't love you half as much as I do. But every single day, you were worth it, and each day without you has been like being murdered over and over again.

The pain taught me something, though. There was another choice. I could've accepted the miracle and blessing of you each second we had together. Then if the day came where a true mate came calling, I could choose the fire and know I lived the best life any man could ask for. It was on my terms."

"Your passing would kill me. That's not a plan, prickly pear. We spent decades with the what-ifs. They were the best decades of my life. I could never watch you die."

He felt Leif smile against his forehead. "Maybe it isn't a good plan, but you forgot about your panic attack, didn't you?"

Aspen pinched Leif's side.

Leif chuckled, completely unbothered.

Aspen's shoulders relaxed. "I don't know what I'm doing anymore."

"Nothing." The lights went out, plunging them into darkness. Even though they could still see as clearly as they could in the daylight, the darkened room brought its own calming effect. Leif buried his hand beneath Aspen's shirt and settled in the way he always had when they slept. "Close your eyes. Let everything go. Every issue will still be there in the morning, but they might not look as heavy once you've had some rest. Okay?"

Aspen nodded. He was in Leif's arms. That was where his happiness had always lived. He would savor what he could get.

Leif stared into the darkness. His mind stewed. Celeste had given him two weeks to win Aspen or lose him forever. Yet Lysander was on the front porch, ripping Stone to shreds, and literally nothing made sense any longer. Lysander had sounded ugly jealous and what the fuck? Did Celeste really intend to pair Aspen with someone obviously involved with someone else? Plus, just ugh. How dare Stone and Lysander bring their bullshit to sweet Aspen's door? His heart was too tender. His life had been too hard even before Leif came kicking his way through it. Leif had been understating every fact when he talked about the pack that had turned its back on Aspen. They were a rowdy bunch of biker bears who lived violent lives. Aspen had been raised in that mess. He meant "raised" in the barest minimum of the word, since they had been abusive as fuck. Nothing pleasant had happened to Aspen before Leif came along. The bear pack had done their best to beat the kindness out of the softest bear alive. All they accomplished was creating a big, overly strong cuddle bug with epic anxiety issues. Aspen had lost nothing when he lost those pieces of shit. But love was complicated, and sometimes good sense had absolutely nothing to do with it. It seemed Aspen had one of those "well, they're my parents" mentality on the matter. He had done a damn good job of hiding that from Leif for decades. Now Aspen was too much of a mess to hide anything. Leif saw every thought and memory. Felt every hurt Aspen hid. Maybe he wasn't what was best for Aspen. It was possible Aspen should just lose himself in the Wulfe pack. Except Celeste intended to pair Aspen with Lysander if Leif didn't act. Every thought he had led back to one: what the fuck?

His bear was a snorer. The sound made Leif smile. Even though there had been times when Leif had wanted to smother him with his pillow over the years, he missed even that now. A true life was a mixture of small irritations with tons of love. At least, the best lives were like that, and they had shared the greatest life. Maybe it was gone now. There was a real possibility there was nothing ahead for them but more heartbreak. Leif hadn't truly survived losing Aspen the first time. He couldn't do that twice in his life, but neither could he give up. Leif just couldn't. Cosmic pairing or not, Aspen had always been the one for him. No amount of heavenly intervention could change that.

Aspen startled so hard in his sleep, he nearly knocked out Leif's fangs. He gasped for air and then focused on Leif with a desperation in his eyes that would have brought Leif to his knees if he had been standing.

You didn't leave.

Leif swallowed all the tears as Aspen's thoughts brushed his brain. *Try to make me.*

For a moment, they simply held each other's gaze. Leif had no clue who moved first, but their mouths hit like they had been starved for each other for years, because they had. His eyes stung as the memories came pouring back. A needy whine slipped out as he recalled all the nights of Aspen's huge cock nearly tearing him in two. He always gave Leif exactly what he begged for, and fuck. Leif wanted it.

Leif had never been more serious about allowing nothing to come between them. The moment he found himself beneath Aspen, Leif threw up his hands and took control of the magic most of the universe never saw. The same magic protecting Frost became the blockade hiding them. No one could ruin them but themselves.

Aspen chuckled against his lips. "What are you doing?"

Leif wasn't one to lie. "Keeping the world out. I've missed you too much to risk the universe turning against us."

"Good thinking." He tore at Lief's clothes.

Leif couldn't stop smiling. He had forgotten how amazing it felt to have Aspen support his decisions. They had always been a team. Leif needed that now. Aspen didn't let him down. The sound of clothes ripping cut through the air.

"Sorry," Aspen mumbled between kisses.

"Fuck that." With a single thought, their clothes disappeared. "Don't hold back." The sensation of their nude bodies touching was such a powerful reminder of their love that Leif could barely breathe. His fangs were past the point of retraction. Leif's body screamed for more. "Please?" Yeah, he begged. Leif didn't fucking care if he looked pathetic. Life had stripped something from him when it took away Aspen. Now he was here, and Leif thought he might die if Aspen didn't make love to him.

Aspen slowed down. He deepened their kiss. "I need your help," Aspen whispered against his lips.

It took a quick glimpse into Aspen's mind to see Aspen didn't own lube any longer. That realization was a punch to the throat, reminding him what true loyalty looked like. What true love looked like.

Leif snapped his fingers, and lube appeared. "I'll always have everything you need."

Aspen stared into his eyes and made no move to continue. Leif wondered if he had ruined the moment somehow. He could practically see the realization growing inside Aspen that this one night meant more than a night of making love. They were reclaiming something maybe best left in the past.

"I never left you in the past. You've always been right here." Aspen tapped his chest. "For me, it's been you or no one."

Everything inside Leif screeched to a halt. "Wait. Did you just read my mind?" Tears streaked from the corners of his eyes, rolling back onto the bed. It was out of his control. "No. Seriously. Did you just read my mind?" He didn't care if he looked hysterical. Leif needed to know.

Aspen swallowed so hard, it looked like it hurt. "I think I did."

Leif didn't hesitate. He didn't give a single fucking thought. Leif simply shot up and buried his fangs in Aspen's throat. He sucked. Leif couldn't think about what would happen to his sanity if no mating mark appeared. The fallout would be too huge to fathom.

The moan Aspen released combined with his emotions overwhelmed Leif. His body jerked as a powerful orgasm overcame him. He felt everything Aspen did, and the experience shook him to his core. Even as he still spit cum, Leif retracted his fangs. He had to know. His entire chest stuttered as he tried to breathe. He couldn't even blink as he watched the wounds heal, leaving behind two perfect round scars. Leif fell apart. He had turned his back on everything, including his Goddess, and now he stared at the biggest blessing a warrior could only dream of having. Despite his abandonment at a time when her nephew disappeared, she had still given Aspen to him.

"Shhh. Don't cry. I still love you. It might still happen one of these days."

Leif realized his mind had turned so chaotic that he had left Aspen in the dark. He didn't understand. Leif shook his head. "No." He swiped his eyes. "You don't... there's a scar."

Aspen turned into a statue. Not a single thought stood out for Leif to see. It was as if shock froze him and wiped him clean. Before Leif saw it coming, Aspen struck, tearing into Leif's throat.

A loud gasp ripped from Leif before another earth-shattering orgasm rocked his soul. The sensation of being stitched together—like a rope in his chest being tethered to Aspen — was a muted thing beneath the pleasure. When Aspen pulled away, blood still covered his lips. He had taken on a slightly bear-like appearance. His gaze stayed glued to Leif's neck. After a moment, he scrambled away and covered his mouth.

Leif took in the vision of him. His dark hair was a mess, and his huge, hairy body was sexy as fuck with his hard cock still dripping with cum. *Goddamn. All that is mine.*

Aspen's gaze finally moved back to hold Leif's stare as he obviously heard Leif's thoughts. His hand dropped from his face. He still looked shaken. "I don't know what to—"

Leif pounced. He swiped his hand through the river of cum coating his stomach and grasped Aspen's dick. Leif stroked him, coating him with the mess before impaling himself. The pain was heaven. A blissful reality check. They were alive. They were one. Biggest of them all, they were mated.

Leif bounced on Aspen's cock, taking what he wanted as he stole the deepest kiss he could get. He wanted to crawl beneath Aspen's skin and never leave. Nothing else mattered. Every memory and ounce of pain led to this moment, and everything was worth it.

I love you. Fuck, Leif. I love you so much. You feel so good. I never want to stop.

Aspen's thoughts matched Leif's. *You'll never want for a single fucking thing. I love you so damn much. You're permanently my cuddly bear. Nothing can break this.*

"I know. Mhmm. Please. It's right there. Come for me. I need—" A strangled cry burst from Aspen, sending Leif flying. He gasped for air simply from the emotional impact.

"Tell me you love me again."

Aspen's arms squeezed him tighter. "I love you." The way the words stuttered from Aspen made Leif realize he was crying.

Leif kissed the tears away. There was nothing either of them could say to express what they felt. Over fifty years together and two years of absolute soul-crushing agony apart, and they had been spun on their heads. Sometimes there were no words yet in creation to describe the power of a moment. But the soul knows and is forever marked. Just as they were now. It was beautiful.

Chapter Four

ASPEN MEANDERED FROM ROOM to room through the house, sipping coffee while Leif slept. Most vampires didn't need sleep at all but chose to keep a schedule because eternity was damn long. Having to fill twenty-four hours every day with activity of some sort had driven some to madness. In Leif's case, he had been born a druid and turned vampire in his twenties to keep himself safe through violent times. Leif hadn't grown fully into his powers by then, and the world was untamed. Everyone woke up with one goal: survive. Leif had done that. Unfortunately, using his magic took a toll. He was one of those rare vampires who slept for a genuine purpose. He was wiped out.

Aspen stopped in the open doorway of one empty room in his new home. His unpacked boxes sat in the open closet. They were there for a reason. The boxes contained the life he had shared with Leif. Aspen had boxed them and stored them, attempting to separate himself from that part of his past. Now he imagined he would unpack them soon. Not today, though. Aspen still reeled and expected the whole mating thing to be a dream. He would wake up any minute, and the pain might actually end him when everything slipped through his fingers.

Aspen moved on, inspecting the home he purchased. The place wasn't huge, but it was paid for, and the woods were nearby. It was a three-bedroom, two-bathroom house. Like nearly everything in Wulfe, the place had been here for a while. It was nearly a hundred years old, but everything was solid and made by hand to last. The house had an old-home smell that brought out all the nostalgia. Not to mention, the place had been built in the day when rooms were huge. At just over two thousand square feet, he didn't feel confined. That was important for a bear his size.

Aspen made his way back to the living room. He had to force his feet to keep moving when they wanted to stop at his bedroom. Leif was all warm and cozy. All Aspen had to do was slip beneath the covers and kiss Leif awake. Leif needed rest. Aspen felt his exhaustion. The last two years had ground Leif down in a way Aspen hadn't expected. He hated himself for the pain he had caused. At the time, there were no good options, and loving Aspen had been destroying Leif.

As Aspen stepped into the living room, he found the most beautiful woman he had ever seen sitting on his couch, openly relaxing. Leif would always be the hottest person alive to him, but he had eyes, and she was stunning.

A smile stretched across her lips at the sight of Aspen. "There you are."

Her voice was mesmerizing. Aspen couldn't explain that. There was just something behind every note. "Um." Aspen rubbed the back of his neck and then looked behind him as if the answer to her presence was hiding somewhere. He focused on the blonde again. She looked slightly familiar, but she was still in his house without invitation. Plus, Leif had warded the house last night. But she was just a tiny thing, and Aspen wasn't, so she couldn't possibly be that big of a threat. Still... "Why are you in my house, and why do you look familiar?"

She waved her hand absently. "Leif's wards faded about an hour ago. He obviously didn't mean for them to be permanent. To answer your second question."

It didn't escape Aspen that she hadn't answered the first.

"I brought you a drink from Leif at the casino after your big win. Kyrie did that for you, by the way. He's a beautiful soul."

There was a lot of information in that speech but no real answers.

She chuckled and patted the cushion next to her. "Come. Sit. I'm Celeste."

Aspen had already taken two steps in her direction, ready to obey with no idea why, when her name hit. He missed a step. His gaze moved over face. Of course, she was. That explained a lot yet nothing at all. He sat and stared at her in awe.

"You're beautiful." Aspen blushed as the words left his lips. It hadn't even been a compliment. He couldn't have stopped that truth from bursting from him if he tried.

She patted his arm. "You're a sweet bear. That's why you've always been destined for Leif. I knew he would protect your peace. Maybe it took me a while to figure out how I could make that happen. But from the day you were born, you were destined to love him."

The sound of Leif's name pulled him from his shock. He smiled. "Thank you for that." He blushed again. He felt exposed sitting next to the goddess he had prayed so hard to, begging for a miracle. Aspen had begged Odin as well, even though he had known Odin had nothing to do with picking mates. It was kind of horrifying. He never thought he would have this meeting, looking directly at the being he had humbled himself so hard for.

After Celeste had patted his arm, she hadn't moved her hand from him. Warmth spread from where she touched him, filling his soul with comfort. "Don't be embarrassed. Love is a serious thing. Some would say it's the most important part of life. Love drives almost every action. Men have started entire wars over that single emotion. You had found it, and—like me—you had no idea how to make it permanent. With that said, you never had to fear either of you finding a mystery mate. If I hadn't found a way, it still would've been the two of you forever."

A huge lump lived in Aspen's throat. He had needed to hear this so many years back. All he had gotten was silence.

"Time moves differently in the heavens," Celeste said, obviously hearing his thoughts. "Also, this is a special case. I don't explain myself to anyone. It's important to me that Leif doesn't think turning his back on me got him his way. Do you understand?"

Aspen nodded. "You wouldn't be safe if people thought all they had to do is walk away from you to get their prayers answered."

Her expression was serious. She meant business. Celeste couldn't let soldiers disobey her. That was dangerous. It made her look weak. "In this case, though, I've been busy. I didn't know how bad the situation had gotten until Leif looked at me with genuine hatred. As cold as it may sound, there are bigger problems right now. However, I wanted to take a minute to talk to you. You have a sweet, soft soul. Leif needs that more than you know. You can see inside him now. Search. You'll know what he hides when you see it."

Celeste suddenly vanished.

Leif ambled into the room still looking tired. Despite the exhaustion in Leif's eyes, he wore a sweet smile. "Good morning, sexy. The bed felt kind of empty."

Aspen couldn't stop smiling. There was a lot of bare chest on display. "I got hungry."

Leif chuckled as he crawled onto the couch and sprawled out, using Aspen's lap as a pillow.

Aspen grabbed the blanket folded on the back of the couch and covered Leif. With Leif settled, Aspen ran his fingers through Leif's hair. The long locks were a mess.

"Mhmm. That feels good."

With Leif's eyes closed, Aspen got to inspect his face without guilt. Leif needed a lot more sleep than Aspen realized. His prickly pear was drained in a way Aspen had never seen before.

"You smell like cotton candy." Leif muttered the words, sounding half asleep. Suddenly, Leif's eyes shot open. "Wait. Why do you smell like heaven?"

Aspen dodged. "How do you know what heaven smells like?"

"I've been there. Don't pretend I didn't ask you—" Leif froze. "Celeste was here. Why was Celeste here?" It seemed he had reached in and taken what he wanted from Aspen.

Leif shook his head. "You know I try not to scoop thoughts from you without your permission. Why was Celeste here?"

Aspen didn't know how to answer. It was obvious Celeste had come to him and not Leif for a reason. He decided to sum things up in a diluted way. "She wanted me to know she'd spent a long time trying to find a way to make us permanent. But she never intended to tear us apart with a random mate. We were written in the stars, apparently."

Leif settled back down. "I can't imagine Celeste explaining herself to anyone ever. It seems her nephew being missing has her more frazzled than I realized."

All thoughts of laziness disappeared. "I don't know who her nephew is, but you're supposed to be a soldier she trusts heavily. Until you walked away, anyhow. You know what I mean. You should be out there helping her." As soon as the words passed his lips, another thought hit. Celeste had told him to take care of Leif. "After you get some more sleep." He urged Leif to relax. Aspen went back to running his fingers through Leif's hair. "You're no good to anyone this exhausted. Just close your eyes. Everything else can wait a few more hours. I've got you."

Leif closed his eyes.

Aspen felt his determination to stay awake. He worried about Aspen's well-being above his. But in no time, Aspen put him to sleep with his tender touches. Aspen smiled at the sight of Leif sleeping on his lap, as if he had never popped up in anger. His gaze moved to the scar everyone would see on Leif's neck. This was his favorite day. Aspen sipped the coffee he had set aside when he sat down with Celeste. He winced. It was cold and needed honey. He had gotten distracted at the grocery store yesterday and forgot to pick some up.

Leif rolled to face him and snuggled closer. He touched the cup Aspen held. Steam rose from the top, yet Leif was asleep.

Aspen took another sip. It was perfect. He wouldn't be surprised if there was a cupboard filled with bottles of honey now too. Aspen couldn't stop staring at his miracle. They had a love so deep, it couldn't be measured or even dampened in their sleep. Aspen had never been more grateful in his life. Whatever darkness Leif hid, Aspen would find it and fix him. That's what mates were for.

In a show of support of Aspen's efforts to become part of the community, Leif went to find Audor while Aspen helped a neighbor with their AC unit. He imagined with Frost in hiding, Audor was free. Leif went to Audor's place first. His house seemed like the most reasonable place to start. Waylon's police cruiser was gone. That made sense. He was likely on duty. Of course, it was equally possible all their vehicles were parked inside the massive detached garage that was twice the size of the house. The sound of hammering led Leif that way. The side door stood open, and a sweat-soaked Audor worked away on a bookcase.

"Hey."

Audor's gaze flickered his way before returning to his work. "Hey. I heard you were back in town."

Damn. Audor was angry with him. It wasn't as if he had left town without leaving a note. Audor should know Leif wouldn't completely abandon their friendship. Still, Leif treaded lightly.

He moved closer and eyed the gorgeous, finished wood pieces nearby. "These look amazing. What has you building up a storm?" Working with his hands was how Audor dealt with stress. He hated the idea that he hadn't been here when Audor obviously needed him. This much furniture surely didn't have a purpose in their home.

"You know me. I can't sit around on my thumbs. With Frost gone, I have a ton of free time. I got the old website up and running again, changed the name, and put out the open for business sign. Tons of orders poured in. I don't know if I can keep up."

Considering Audor was a vampire who could move at speeds unseen by the naked eye, that said a lot.

"Wow. I'm glad to hear it's a success. At least it's not like the good ole days of having to fake an entire life again, retiring, and having a son take over the business."

"That shit did get tiring." He finally stopped working and focused on Leif. His gaze immediately moved to the mating mark. "Wait. Is this...? Are you and Aspen...?"

A bright smile exploded across Leif's face. He had known Audor wouldn't stay angry for long. "Yeah."

Audor turned into the giant child he could be. "Yes!" He bounced up and down a few times before barreling toward Leif. If Leif had been a lesser vamp, he would've been taken to the ground from Audor's enthusiasm. He hugged Leif and bounced again, taking Leif with him. "Yes! Yes! I'm so happy. Oh, my Goddess. This is so, so amazing. No one deserves this more than you two. I can't believe it."

Even though he smiled so hard at Audor's excitement that his face hurt, Leif pushed at Audor's chest. "Ewww. You're all sweaty and stuff." Leif knew he sounded like as big of a kid as Audor did. They were dumb when they were together. It was like they lowered each other's IQ by at least five points. "Save all that nastiness for Waylon."

"Did I hear my name?" Waylon stepped through the door. While he smiled at their antics, he also looked confused by them.

Audor released Leif, but he didn't stop bouncing on his toes. "Look!" He stabbed a finger toward Leif's neck, nearly taking out Leif's eye in the process. "He has a fucking mating mark. I'm so excited."

Waylon's gaze slid his way. His smile didn't dampen. "Who? You'd better say Aspen? Otherwise, I'll have to get my ass kicked by you on behalf of my pack. I can't have you out here betraying a pack member."

Leif laughed. He didn't take the threat to heart. "Yeah, it's Aspen."

Waylon's smile grew. "That's really good to hear. I can't believe I got the hottest town tea firsthand. This never happens to me."

The way Audor smiled as he looked between them warmed Leif's heart. He felt the happiness pulsing from the couple. Audor had been blessed with an excellent mate. That mattered to Leif.

Leif accepted a handshake from Waylon before he pivoted topics. "Now that I've ensured the news will reach everyone in town."

"Are you calling me a gossip?" Waylon clutched his chest in a dramatic show. "I'm hurt."

Audor snagged Waylon's belt loop and tugged him closer. "No, you're not. You can't wait to get out of here and tell everyone." He never stopped smiling even as he stole a kiss from his mate.

Waylon pulled away. "You're right. I never get to be first. I'm taking full advantage."

Leif laughed at Waylon's genuine excitement. "My late mating gift to you. Feel free to use your megaphone and everything."

They chuckled before Leif turned things to the serious side. "Tell me what's happening with Frost missing." While Leif didn't know exactly where Frost stayed now, he knew Frost was safe. His concern was about the shakeup Frost had caused.

Audor's hands rose and fell. "The demon Lucifer put in place at the ER is holding his own. Frost's pack clients seemed to be oddly fine."

"I don't know what'll happen when those babies decide they want out. A lot of these folks came here just for the shot at bringing a pup safely into the world. Without Frost..." Waylon shook his head. "I don't know, but I haven't heard a whisper of fear amongst the pack. Honestly, the entire situation is strange."

Leif fought the urge to fidget and give himself away. He felt guilty as hell knowing something they didn't when it was this important. "I have faith. Frost is powerful and kind. I can't imagine him allowing any harm to come to anyone."

Audor backhanded Leif's chest. "I forgot." He focused on Waylon. "Leif here is pretty damn powerful too. I mean, he's not trained as a healer. But if push comes to shove, I'm sure there's something he can do to help if babies start popping out."

Audor's speech gave Leif the excuse he needed to shift from one foot to the other. A nervous laugh escaped him. "Um, yeah. I'm not sure about that. Like you said, I'm not a healer. Everything I can do is basically a parlor trick."

"Bullshit." Audor was always his biggest cheerleader behind Aspen. "You kept me alive until Frost could reattach my leg."

"Barely." It seemed Audor needed to clear his memory. "You lost so much blood, I doubt you remember much of anything that happened." In truth, Leif had panicked. When Lucifer had caught them trailing him, Leif was certain they were dead. Lucifer plucked Audor's leg off like it was a butterfly wing. Leif had snatched Audor and his leg and zapped them to the nearest empty cabin. Then he had basically kidnapped Frost and forced him to save Audor. Nothing he could be proud of happened that night. Now he was thrilled Audor had survived with all his limbs, but he hadn't done the work. That was Frost. Leif stayed far away from the magic hero business. The first rule of any healer was to first do no harm. Leif was a walking disaster.

Waylon chimed in. “It’s funny. I’ve always smelled magic around you, but I didn’t realize it’s actually you. I thought it was just your being with Frost all day. But I smell it now. I can’t believe I missed it. You’re more than half druid. Well, now I’m just confused.”

Audor answered before Leif could. “Leif was born a druid. He was turned vampire. I’m no expert in biology or anything, but I think he’s still technically full druid. He just happens to also be a vampire.”

Audor always sounded so proud when he talked about Leif. It was nice. Sometimes, there would be a moment that reminded him how close they were. He loved Audor like a brother. They were best friends.

"I'm sorry I worried you." At his veer off topic, Audor focused on him with his eyebrows raised. Leif pressed on. "I never dreamed you'd think you'd never see me again. Please know I'd never do that to you. You're the only person I have beyond Aspen." Leif knew he had chosen an odd moment to bare his heart, but he couldn't let Audor go even a moment longer thinking Leif could abandon him.

To his surprise, tears filled Audor's eyes. He visibly swallowed before he spoke. "I've spent a lot of nights sick to my stomach, thinking about how my being fated for a wolf drove you away. I hate that seeing me with Waylon hurt you. But I didn't know what to say or do to help."

To Leif's horror, a tear slid down his cheek. "I'm so sorry I made you feel guilty for being happy. You deserve your blessings. The problem was always me. Not you."

Audor swiped his eyes and hugged Leif again. This time, Leif didn't try to get away. Sweat and all, Leif needed this hug. When he pulled away after a few hard back pats, he noticed Waylon was gone.

Leif swiped his eyes. "Sorry. I didn't mean to run off your man."

"You didn't. He's in my head, rubbing his hands together about getting the drop on everyone." A loud laugh burst from Audor. He covered his mouth, but his eyes still swam with humor.

"What?"

Even not knowing what happened, Leif still smiled. Audor's happiness was contagious.

Audor dropped his hand. He wore a luminous smile. "Aspen's neighbor Betty Anne already told everyone. The litany of cursing in my head is epic. It seems Aspen went over to help her with her AC and she saw Aspen's mark. It was off to the races the moment he left to see how fast she could spread the word."

Leif couldn't stop smiling. He hadn't known how much happiness he missed just from letting jealousy beat him. Leif also hadn't known this much bliss existed. All he knew was it sounded like Aspen was home. A quick skim of Aspen's mind confirmed his suspicions. He couldn't get to him fast enough.

Chapter Five

ASPEN STOOD AT THE kitchen counter, staring into space and eating cookies. Betty Anne was a sweet lady. As a young, unmated wolf, she couldn't afford to live on her own if she lived anywhere else. Only the small-town pack, helping each other, kept her afloat. The more he thought about their conversation while he worked, the more he realized exactly how horrible life had been here for Kyrie. While this pack was a mixed bag of various Weres, Kyrie was too different, it seemed. Each day that passed, and the more he learned, the closer he felt to the best friend he had made. Aspen had been the odd man out—the outcast of his pack back home. Truthfully, Aspen felt a tad torn. Everyone seemed so nice and accepting. He didn't understand. Kyrie deserved better. He didn't like the way he had been so easily accepted when such a sweet wolf was a pariah.

A warm caress ran through his hair. *Are you okay, sweet bear? I swear I felt you thinking of me in sadness.*

Aspen's chest warmed. He felt a loving smile cross his lips. *Sorry. I just miss you. Are you having fun? Is your honeymoon all things awesome?*

Kyrie's caress moved to Aspen's shoulders as if an invisible hug squeezed him. *It's great. I love it here in Scotland, but I can come back if you need me.*

Aspen rushed to stop that from happening. Kyrie deserved this break from life. *No, enjoy your time with Fen. You two deserve this. I'll still be here when you get back.*

I love you.

Aspen felt all cuddly inside. *I love you too.*

"Who are you exchanging I love yous with, and should I be concerned?"

Aspen startled as Leif appeared behind him. "Holy shit! You need a bell or something."

A sexy chuckle rumbled behind his ear.

Aspen's eyes fell closed as Leif reached past him and took a cookie. Lips brushed the shell of his ear. “Do I get an ‘I love you’ too?”

Fuck. He forgot what they talked about. “I love you.”

“Mmm. That never gets old.” Leif kissed his neck. He pulled away and took a bite. “Oh, that’s good. Homemade?”

Aspen had to take a steadying breath through his nose. His body knew his mate stood only inches away. “Yeah. Betty Anne—”

The sound of a cellphone ringing brought Aspen up short. He spun in a circle. Aspen had no clue where his phone was. It wasn’t like anyone ever called him.

Leif found it first. “It’s a Montana area code.”

For a moment, they stared at each other in silence while phone continued ringing. It fell silent.

“I probably should’ve answered that.”

Leif’s lip curled. “Why?”

Before Aspen could decide why he felt obligated, the phone rang again. Again, neither of them moved.

Leif broke first. “On speaker.”

Aspen gave him a sharp nod. That was for the best. He answered and immediately switched it to speakerphone. “Hello?”

“Rumor is you’ve come into some money. You know whatever belongs to one pack member belongs to the whole pack.”

Aspen's chest immediately ached. His dad hadn't even said hello. In fact, Aspen hadn't heard the man's voice in years.

Leif jumped in, giving Aspen zero time to cave. "Aspen isn't part of your pack." Leif's voice dripped with malice. He sounded deadlier than Aspen had ever heard before. "He's my mate. My family. That supersedes any ties he had to you. Don't call here again."

"Ah. So you came running back the second he struck it rich, huh? Useless leech."

Leif rolled his eyes. *You know damn well that's not true, right?*

Aspen melted as the words brushed his brain. *I know you don't need money. You're my mate. This is love. Always has been.* Aspen's spine stiffened. He might be soft, but he wasn't weak. "You heard my mate. Don't call here again. You chose to turn your back on me. Now live with the consequences." He disconnected the call and turned off the phone before it could ring again. For a moment, he stared at nothing. He had to push the pain down. As much as Aspen knew he didn't owe his old pack a single damn thing, it was hard to know his family didn't love him. That never got easier to carry.

Leif took Aspen's phone and set it aside. He towed Aspen into his arms and held him. His lips brushed Aspen's temple. "I love you. You have me, and you have a new pack. I know it's not the same as having your parents and brother, but you're better off here."

Aspen knew all of that. Some hurts just ran too deep. "I love you too. Don't worry. I'll be okay."

"It's my job to worry." He kissed Aspen's forehead and didn't move. *You still didn't tell me who you're saying I love you to. Mentally, at that. Isn't that supposed to be my thing?*

An exasperated laugh escaped Aspen. "It was Kyrie. You could've looked in my head and seen that."

Leif's lips shaped a smile against Aspen's skin. *I love the sound of your voice.* Belying his claim, Aspen felt Leif shifting through his mind. *I'll be damned. Freyr is still out here making kids? Damn. Kyrie must be a fierce wolf, then. Freyr is a lover and also very much a fighter. He's huge. Kyrie is so tiny. I never would've seen the resemblance.*

Aspen pulled away enough to see Leif's face. "That's the second time today you've spoken like you know too much about the heavens."

Leif shrugged. "I've been around a long time." He twisted and backed Aspen against the counter.

Aspen wouldn't be dodged. "No. You forget how many years we spent together. This is new. Earlier, you said you'd been there."

Aspen poked a little at Leif's brain. He didn't want secrets in their relationship. A solid wall of black met him—like Leif had thrown up a barrier between them.

“Oh.” Even Aspen heard the massive pain in that one word. There was only one reason Leif wouldn’t let him see his thoughts. There was someone else. Likely someone associated with the heavens. Aspen swallowed. He tried to breathe. No oxygen came. The harder he tried, the less air he got. Aspen stared at the floor. He heard Leif talking, but the words were too muffled by the sound of his pulse pounding in his ears. There was no air. Why was there no air?

The world flipped. The scenery changed. He went from staring at the floor to gazing at the ceiling. Aspen couldn’t lie and say he hadn’t seen himself going out this way. But he had always believed it would be losing Leif that did him in. No way could he have imagined this oxygen-deprived death would come after the miracle of their mating. Here he was, though. He felt the life bleeding from him. A blurry image of Leif hovered above him. His lips moved, but Aspen was beyond hearing. Aspen's body had given up. Suddenly, Leif went soaring through the air to a destination he couldn't see. Aspen wasn't even curious. Nothing would matter soon.

"Fucking breathe, Aspen!"

The words cut through the invisible noose around his neck. His vision cleared enough for Aspen to realize it was Kyrie screaming at him.

"That's it, sweetie. Slow down. Take smaller breaths. You can do it."

Aspen followed the sound of Kyrie's voice and matched the pattern of his breathing. The room cleared a little more every second. Kyrie's bright yellow eyes glowed more than ever as he held Aspen's stare. "I've got you, angel. Just keep breathing."

As the room came even more into view, so too did the reason he was in this position. His lungs might work again, but so did his heart, and it was shattered. The tears came fast and hard.

Kyrie moved Aspen into a seated position, leaning him back against the dishwasher. He held Aspen's hand and rubbed it, soothing him. "Talk to me. There's too much pain for me to see anything else."

Aspen still couldn't see anything except Kyrie. He couldn't talk. There was an anvil on his throat.

Fen appeared over Kyrie's shoulder. He urged Kyrie to his feet. "Come on, wee one. It's his mate's right to handle this."

Kyrie looked torn, but he let himself get pulled away. "If you need me, I'm always a shout away. I don't—"

Fen rubbed Kyrie's arms. "Seriously, love. This is one of those times where you can't help."

Kyrie looked like a fish out of water. It was obvious leaving went against his every instinct. He couldn't argue with Fen's logic. With one last heartbreaking look, Kyrie and Fen vanished.

Leif dropped into the spot Kyrie had vacated. He stared at his lap, looking as heartbroken as Aspen felt. His hair was a mess from whatever tumble he endured while Aspen's anxiety took him out.

Aspen's mind was a blank slate. He was too terrified to think. Everything inside him hurt too much. If as much as a centimeter budged in any direction in his mind, he would shatter.

"It's not someone else."

Aspen crossed his arms, trying to physically hold himself together. He stared at Leif. Aspen had never loved anyone so much. They were mates now. Connected for eternity, for the good or the bad. He had never understood why this one person could cause him so much irreparable harm with a single misplaced word or deed. Aspen didn't understand why Leif didn't see how diminished Aspen had become without him. How weak.

Leif set his hand on Aspen's leg and rubbed, but he still didn't meet Aspen's stare. "Last night, when I said there was another choice I could've made—a hypothetical choice—I was just being weak, and testing your reaction, I guess." Leif cleared his throat. His chin lifted and their gazes met. Leif's eyes were blood red and red-rimmed. He hurt too. Aspen felt the pain as if it were a physical touch.

"You can tell me anything." Aspen's voice sounded as if he had spent twelve hours wailing at the top of his lungs.

Leif visibly swallowed. The act had Aspen's gaze dropping to Leif's neck. There was Aspen's mark. His mark. Leif belonged to him, and Aspen couldn't watch him ache.

"You can say it."

Leif took a shaky-sounding breath. "It wasn't a random backup plan. I did it."

Aspen's insides froze. "You did what?" He needed there to be no misunderstandings.

Guilt passed over Leif's features. "You said you didn't want us anymore, but there was no me without you. I walked into the fire."

Aspen gasped. He automatically drew his knees up and covered his mouth, as if everything inside him recoiled.

Leif swallowed again. "Except Celeste wouldn't let me die. Well, she wouldn't let me stay dead. That's why I've been so angry with her. I made my way to peace in heaven. But she still needed me to be the soldier, and—truth be told—as much as I am so fucking thankful for you, I'm still angry. You're my everything. I didn't want to go on without you, and she made me."

Tears rolled down Aspen's cheeks, but he let Leif say all the words.

Leif blinked as if he fought tears and he wouldn't look directly at Aspen. "The pain was unimaginable, and I don't mean the fire. It was like you were ripped away from me, and I couldn't do it. But she needed a fucking soldier, so my suffering meant nothing." He finally met Aspen's stare, and Aspen saw the pain and rage. "I know everything worked out and I'm sitting here now, mated to the only thing in this world I can't live without. Not just the only person, but every goddamn thing I can't live without." Leif's voice shook with emotion. "I know I'm supposed to accept that some grand plan came together in the end. But we were told we could choose a warrior's death, and it's all bullshit. I'm ecstatic to be alive now and sitting here with you. But back then, it was an impossible dream, and she ripped away my only option for comfort."

There was no way Aspen could have known how much pure anger lived inside Leif. Sadness engulfed him. "If you feel that way about her, I can't imagine how you really feel about me. I mean, when I got into town and saw you again for the first time, you looked at me with a loathing I can't even describe. Now you're stuck with me, and...." Aspen's hands rose and fell. "I'm sorry for existing, I guess. You never deserved to have me as a plague on your life. If you'd never met me, you'd—"

"Be the most miserable bastard on the face of the planet," Leif interjected, likely saving Aspen from words he couldn't unsay.

Aspen deflated. He thought he had felt defeated before, but knowing he was the reason Leif had done such a terrible and dumb thing. That was too heavy for him to carry.

Leif scooted closer and touched his lips to Aspen's. "None of this matters now, baby." He kissed Aspen again. His voice remained soft. "Please stop hating me over this." Another sweet kiss swept across his lips. "I just want to leave the past behind and—for once—finally get to enjoy the love we found. Why does everything keep stepping between us? We're supposed to be happy to be mates."

That last bit hit Aspen hard. "I am happy knowing you're mine. I begged for you." In all the line of embarrassing things to say, Aspen didn't feel like admitting the way he had pleaded didn't even make the top fifty on the list. But that was the admission that mattered most now. He stared at his biggest dream come true. That was why it hurt so badly to find out he was Leif's worst nightmare.

In all his life, and it had been a very long existence, Leif had never felt pain like what Aspen experienced. The instant Leif closed his mind to Aspen, Aspen had crumbled. Too late, Leif realized how close Aspen had been to shattering, purely from the way Leif had looked at him the first time he saw Aspen again. There had been nothing left inside Aspen but a thin and cracked veneer of hope for the future when he came after

Leif. Then Leif had taken a baseball bat to Aspen's slowly healing heart.

Leif's hands shook. There was a person-sized hole in the wall where Kyrie had sent him flying through it. He didn't even know how he felt about that because the shock of everything was so thick. All he knew was Aspen couldn't leave him.

"I'm not leaving you."

The statement made the air in Leif's lungs stutter. He heard and felt the shaky breath that escaped him.

"Come here." Aspen pulled Leif onto his lap. Sitting between Aspen's knees, Aspen urged him to lean against his chest before wrapping his arms around Leif in a tight hug.

Leif's eyes closed. He savored the moment. This was one of the things he had missed the most. Aspen was his cuddly bear for a reason. Being in his arms was Leif's version of heaven.

"Do you remember the first place we lived? The one-room cabin in the middle of the woods."

Leif smiled. His eyes stayed shut as he savored the sound of Aspen's voice and warmth of his arms surrounding him. "That place was tiny, especially for a bear."

"I loved it there. You couldn't escape me."

Leif took a breath. With every passing second, the fear and pain lessened. "In those days, we didn't have much in the way of entertainment in the middle of nowhere." A devilish smile tugged at Leif's lips. "But I was never bored."

"Maybe that's what we need."

Leif's eyes opened. He glanced over his shoulder. "To fuck? I'm in."

Aspen chuckled. "That's not what I meant." He paused for a beat. "Or maybe I did. Everything seemed so simple back then. No electronics. Just us with no one else around. We didn't worry about running into a mystery mate. You created a magic little bubble for us so we'd be safe from any chance of a stranger—man or beast—stumbling in. No one existed but us. I don't recall why we ever left."

"Your pack." Leif hated saying those words and ruining the moment, but that was what happened. "You worried they might need you."

"No."

At Aspen's denial, Leif started to argue that was absolutely what had them leaving that bubble.

Aspen continued before Leif could get irritated. "I worried they would tear my little brother to pieces without me around. He was so small and sweet. You know how they felt about anything small or sweet. One day, I woke up and just had the worst feeling in my gut—like I needed to get to him. Not that they let me see him when we returned."

Leif searched his mind, trying hard to remember that part. "I don't recall any of this. Maybe my brain got scrambled in that fire."

A very bear-like growl rumbled against his ear.

"Don't joke about that. Noted."

Aspen licked his neck.

Leif's entire body lit. He had not forgotten this part. The affectionate bear kisses that always stole his breath.

"None of this is the point. Maybe we need to disappear into a bubble again for a little while."

Leif desperately wanted those days back, but he had to be realistic. "I thought you wanted to be part of Waylon's pack. You sacrificed everything for me back then. I don't want you to do that twice. You have no idea how fucking sorry I am for hurting you again. I don't want to make all the same mistakes. Fuck, Aspen. I just want to love you like you deserve."

Aspen licked his neck again. This time, he didn't stop.

Leif's walls fell as all the stress seeped from him. His entire being focused on that tongue. He felt Aspen poking around in his mind, but he couldn't bring himself to care. His skin tingled. Leif's erection grew.

Aspen palmed Leif's dick through his jeans and massaged.

Leif's entire ass left the floor trying to fuck that hand. He needed the release. In one swift motion, Leif was on his back on the kitchen floor. His shirt ripped away as Aspen licked his torso. The way his tongue swirled held every ounce of Leif's focus.

"That feels so good. I've woken up twisted in the sheets over memories of that tongue."

A very animalistic sound rumbled from Aspen's throat. Leif gasped at the sensation. He felt everything like his nerve response had been turned up by a thousand percent. Leif had been rendered useless by Aspen's ministrations. The sound of ripping jeans filled his ears while Aspen traced a circle around Leif's navel. The second air brushed his erection, Aspen's tongue lapped him front root to tip before Aspen swallowed him.

Leif dove his fingers into Aspen's hair. He couldn't even see clearly anymore. The lust was bigger than everything, killing any sense not needed to enjoy Aspen on his dick. He panted as Aspen did his best to suck the skin from Leif's cock. The closer he was pulled toward oblivion, the wilder he turned. He lifted his hips in perfect rhythm with Aspen bobbing on his dick. Leif fucked Aspen's throat. The animalistic noises coming from Aspen were like a vibrator around his cock. Leif couldn't think. Nothing existed but them. When he blew, Leif saw stars and lost all ability to breathe. A silent scream poured from him as he saw stars. He shook with the power of his orgasm. They weren't broken. They were flawless together. Leif would make Aspen remember that.

Chapter Six

RATHER THAN RETURNING TO his duties, Leif spent every day working at Aspen's side. They integrated themselves into the community, helping and simply enjoying the company. They went to bonfires and joined the full moon run. Leif adored watching Aspen's happiness grow by the day. He fit here, and Leif loved that for him. Still, Leif was grateful as hell for a day at home with no plans.

Sprawled out on the couch with his feet on Aspen's lap, Leif stared at Aspen. Aspen rubbed Leif's feet. Leif realized he had intentionally forgotten these moments. Aspen had always quietly spoiled the fuck out of him, treating him like a king. The most addicting part was Aspen didn't even recognize his actions as spoiling him. Aspen loved taking care of Leif in every way. He took pride in it. That was why losing him had literally killed him. There was no life after this one. Everything without Aspen was too hard. When Celeste had sent him back, Leif had been forced to convince himself he hated Aspen. Without that shield of anger and loathing, life was too crippling. Now here he was, staring into the face of ultimate happiness. He wished he knew how to make Aspen feel just as cherished.

“If you could have anything, no matter how outlandish it is, what would you want?”

Aspen looked his way. His expression screamed that he took the inquiry seriously. “Hmm.” He laughed and shook his head, as if his first thought was absurd.

“What?” Leif couldn’t stop smiling. He knew he could read Aspen’s mind. But he had realized a lifetime ago how much he loved the anticipation of what Aspen might say next. It was rare for him to dive into Aspen’s thoughts. This was a hell of a lot more fun.

A slight blush tinted Aspen’s cheeks.

Leif had never been so excited to hear an answer.

Aspen chuckled. "My first thought was how cute it would be if we had an actual bear cave. A love nest." Aspen made a dismissive gesture. "Not like a gross hole in a hill, but a little getaway—like a hobbit house, but big enough for a bear." He shook his head again. "I'm not making sense."

"That's not true. I can practically see the place in my head."

Leif felt Aspen brush his thoughts, as if he didn't want to be rude, and only wanted a peek.

Aspen's smile grew. "Yeah. Just like that. A little cozy yet hidden spot where no one can bother us. We can take little breaks from society." His gaze turned heated. "A place where I can do whatever I want to you, and no one can hear you scream."

Leif's breath caught at the heat in Aspen's eyes. He felt his expression shift to seductive. Aspen was the perfect mixture of achingly sweet and naughty as hell. In all their years together, Leif hadn't once tired of him. If anything, the cravings got worse year by... Damn. The lust *had* only grown. How had he been so blind? Leif had lived in agony all because he couldn't have Aspen's mark. He had been so focused on that, Leif hadn't stopped to think. There was only one reason they would spend decades together and never get bored. He had been distraught to the point of stepping into the fire. How had he not recognized his soul ripping into two pieces? Leif was floored. Somehow, without the mark or any of the normal pathways, they had always been soulmates.

"I regret nothing, you know?"

Leif startled at Celeste's sudden appearance. Aspen didn't react. In fact, he sat frozen, as if a movie on pause.

Leif's gaze swung back Celeste's way. "Have you taken up voyeurism?"

A beautiful laugh filled the air. Celeste's eyes twinkled. "It's my job to watch. Obviously, I have my own life and whatnot, but I'm always around somewhere."

He wanted to be comfortable with Celeste. Leif wanted to forgive her. "What is that life? What do you do in the heavens all day?"

"Odin."

Celeste answered without missing a beat, causing an unexpected laugh to burst from Leif. “Really?”

Celeste shrugged. “He’s my other half, so yeah. Warriors come with warrior stamina.” Her bright smile never dimmed throughout the confession. “By the way, it’s okay if you’re still angry. You can’t see everything the way I can.”

A hint of guilt wormed its way into his soul. While he would never betray Frost, he still recognized Celeste should know. He tried like hell to keep his thoughts locked behind a wall.

Celeste made a dismissive gesture. “The day you came back to town and disappeared, you solidified a theory I had. Frost’s patients were still well cared for, so I had a feeling he was still around.

If he's safe, then that's all I can ask for right now."

Damn. He didn't stand a chance against her. Leif focused on Aspen to stop any other thoughts that might get him in trouble. His heart melted. "He really is perfect, isn't he?"

"Agreed. My sweet Odin did a great job when he created Aspen. His heart is solid gold. That's why you have to protect it."

There was something in her tone that had Leif's gaze swinging back her way.

Celeste held his stare. "His family is almost here. Aspen needs his warrior now."

Before he could say another word, Celeste vanished. The world restarted. Aspen shifted positions, as if he meant to climb on top of Leif. A loud knock took the front door off its hinges. Leif sprang into action. In a heartbeat, he was on his feet, in full Viking dress and mode. With a battle ax in each hand, Leif blocked their path.

Fury bled from him. "How dare you beat down Aspen's door?"

"Our door," Aspen said quietly at Leif's back. He curled his fingers around the waistband of Leif's pants. Leif swept an internal gaze across Aspen's mind. Aspen held on for protection. Not to keep Leif from fighting.

Bernard's light brown eyes matched Aspen's, except there was no kindness in them. His eyes were flat and dead. There was nothing inside but greed and evil. "I suggest you step aside, tiny Viking. You may be strong, but you're not pack-of-grizzlies strong. You're in the way."

Aspen's grip tightened.

Leif braced his feet and readied his axes. "Make me move, bitch."

Bernard's features shifted just enough to warn Leif he was about to strike.

"I clearly remember directing you out of town."

Bernard swung around at the shout behind him. Waylon and fifteen other members of the Wulfe pack stood in the yard. He was in his sheriff's gear with his hands on his hips, as if ready to pull his gun.

Aspen moved to Leif's side and clung to his arm.

Bernard swapped targets. "You're not the alpha of this group. I am." Malice dripped from Bernard's lips.

Waylon wore a friendly smile even as he radiated power and danger. "Now, you know damn well that's not true."

Leif exchanged a glance with Aspen. This was new information.

"I'm alpha of the entire northwest. You're just some bear playacting."

Grumbles rumbled among the bear pack.

Bernard's rage practically crackled from him. "Don't toy with me, wolf. I'm here for one of mine. If I have to tread through you to get to him, I will."

Leif pushed Aspen back to stand behind him. "You won't live long enough to reach him."

Bernard never acknowledged Leif. His focus was officially stolen by the wolf claiming to be his alpha. Leif could see his every thought. He fully intended to leave here with a tattered Aspen and all of Aspen's money. But he would be damned if he left here with anyone thinking they were above him. If he didn't have a full chokehold on his bears, he knew the hardened grizzlies would never bow to him.

"No bear will ever bow to a wolf." He took a step in Waylon's direction.

Frost and Gemini literally appeared out of nowhere at Waylon's side. "What's going on here? Is everything okay?" Frost held his doctor's bag. His entire demeanor screamed concern.

Every head turned Frost's way.

Bernard obviously saw his chance. He ran and leapt, seemingly intent on catching Waylon off guard.

Frost's eyes widened. His arm shot out. It was like everything happened in the blink of an eye yet still in slow motion. Like he was nothing but a tiny bird, Frost snatched Bernard from the air and tossed him to the ground. He easily held him down while Bernard swiped at Frost's legs. Frost's power was on full display. It was beyond obvious Frost's hold kept Bernard from shifting and his blows were like butterflies landing on Frost's legs.

"For Goddess' sake. What in the—"

A loud roar rent the air, making the ground shake, and cutting off Frost. Lucifer appeared like a wraith of fury. His eyes were solid black, and his fangs were on full display. Bernard was ripped from Frost's hold. Lucifer held Bernard in the air with one arm—like a rag doll. "You attacked my son." It wasn't a scream. Lucifer's words were growled in a chilling tone that made the hair stand up on the back of Leif's neck.

As someone who witnessed Lucifer pluck Audor's leg from his body, this was still the most terrifying thing Leif ever witnessed. Everyone was frozen. Fear clogged the air. No one wanted to move and catch Lucifer's attention. But Leif could practically feel the way everyone wanted to look at Frost at Lucifer's words.

Lucifer's voice turned even scarier. "No one touches my son." With the smallest of shakes, Bernard vanished. He simply wasn't there any longer. Lucifer turned his ire Frost's way. He pointed at Frost. "You." He pointed at Gemini. "And you. Let's go."

While Gemini and Frost exchanged glances, they didn't argue. They followed Lucifer's lead, and the three disappeared together.

"Where did he go?" The bears shifted uneasily and looked at each other like they had no idea what to do now. "Do we go look for him or what?"

Another confused bear shrugged. "I mean, where do we even start?"

"Oh, he's *dead*, dead," Leif said, breaking things down for them.

"You've got thirty minutes to get out of my town."

The bear pack jumped as if startled. This time, they didn't hesitate to move their asses at Waylon's command. The remaining bears rushed down the stairs. Bullies were useless without their leader.

"Well, I've officially seen it all."

A laugh burst from Leif at Aspen's claim. His tone was funny as hell. Aspen wrapped his arms around Leif and set his chin on Leif's shoulder. "I haven't seen you in this outfit in a long time. Your ass looks amazing in leather."

Leif shook his head. It had been one hell of a day. Yet—somehow—Aspen still made Leif smile.

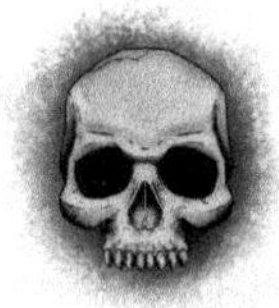

Aspen knew he should feel some sort of way about very likely witnessing his father's death. He didn't. Bernard had meant less than nothing to him for a damn long time. He was practically a stranger. A cruel stranger. Aspen felt terrible about causing a fuss, though. He had just moved to town and already his presence stirred up trouble.

Aspen kissed Leif's neck. "Give me a second. I need to talk to Waylon."

Leif stepped aside, making room for Aspen to pass.

While flashing as much heat as possible, Aspen touched Leif way more than necessary to slip past him.

Tease.

Aspen's gaze dropped to Leif's mouth. *Never.* With promise still lingering between them, Aspen headed Waylon's way. "Thank you for showing up. I can't tell you how sorry I am. While I haven't been a part of my dad's pack for decades, as soon as he learned I had something to take, he turned up like the bad penny he is. He's always been a bastard."

Waylon didn't look upset in the least. His amber eyes held a kindness Aspen had never seen in an alpha. "You have nothing to be sorry about. The people here are falling in love with you. This is what real packs do. We have each other's backs."

Several people still milled around, nodding their heads.

Aspen shifted from foot to foot. Now that the focus was totally on him, his nerves set in. He glanced around. "Thank you all for showing up. I didn't mean to bring this mess here."

A lot of 'don't worry about it' and 'no big deals' got tossed around. There was more unrest about Lucifer, and if Frost was okay, than Aspen's dad. Aspen felt like he had whiplash from all the things happening since he had come to town.

Aspen listened to the worried mumbling for a moment. He focused on Waylon again. "What do you need me to do?"

"No matter how you felt about the guy, I'm sure this business with your father is a lot to deal with right now. Focus on yourself today. This town will still be here after you've had time to process."

Audor sidled up to Waylon's side. "All possible human witnesses have been checked. They already have no memory of this. I assume that's Lucifer's doing.

No one else here is powerful enough to make so many people see nothing."

"Well, there's that," Waylon said, sounding exhausted.

Audor kissed Waylon. It was sweet. Aspen automatically turned his head to let them have their moment. "I have to go look for Frost. It's my duty."

Leif joined them, obviously overhearing everything with his supernatural hearing. "I should go too."

Aspen pressed his lips together for a moment to stop himself from smiling too hard. He had felt Leif in his head. Leif knew Aspen was genuinely fine. His willingness to return to his duties for Celeste gave Aspen more hope and peace than he wanted to admit. He needed Leif to be healed. "You should. Audor might need the help."

Aspen was thankful when Audor didn't argue at his urging. It was possible he, too, wanted Leif's bitterness to slip into nothing but faded memory.

Leif stole a kiss from Aspen. *Raincheck on that teasing.*

Aspen's smile was back. He was so fucking happy. Even the drama of the day couldn't shake him. *I'll be waiting.*

Leif kissed him again and then fell into step with Audor, heading for a near-by truck. It seemed they would trav-el the old-fashioned way until the sun set. Aspen got it. Leif couldn't let the whole town know how powerful he was. Druids were too rare and highly sought. Frost had been assigned protection. No such thing was extended to Leif. He was a warrior. Aspen supposed no one saw him as a man who lived in fear.

Waylon squeezed his shoulder, pulling Aspen's attention back his way. "Are you sure you're okay? You know it's more likely than not your father is gone. Lucifer doesn't take hostages. I hate to sound so blunt, but I don't want to leave here if you need someone to lean on."

Aspen was moved. This was what a real pack looked like. It was beautiful. He had to clear his throat to respond. "The word 'father' has never meant anything to me. As the alpha, my dad just chose whomever he wanted to mate with, and my brother and I are the product of that. From the day we were born, we were given nothing. The moment he could rip us from a loving mother, he did. From there, we either survived, or we didn't. I likely have many siblings who didn't."

Waylon shook his head. "Unfortunately, it's a story I've heard before. We have a few townspeople who ended up here the same way. You know your father wasn't an alpha, right?"

Aspen nodded. "Yeah, but it doesn't matter if it's true or not when you live in a secluded area, kept away from anyone who could challenge his self-given title. He was the meanest, and people were scared to go against him." Aspen shrugged. "They're a gang, and he was the leader. My only hope is my brother is still out there, untainted by Bernard. If so, maybe he'll find me one day. I'm not up for the heartache of knowing he's gone—through death or brainwashing."

"I get it."

Aspen took a step back. "I should let you get back to work. All this shit has wiped me out. I think I need to sleep off some of this stress."

Waylon chuckled and took a step back in the direction of his parked patrol car. "Bears and their naps." The crowd had dispersed. There was no reason to linger. "Call me if you need anything. I'll keep watch to make sure those guys leave town."

Aspen smiled, and they said their goodbyes. By the time Aspen made it inside and closed the door against the world, he was ready to collapse. He was just so damn mentally exhausted. Aspen turned the lock and headed for the couch. He would grab a quick nap before Leif got home. Waylon was right. Bears loved to sleep. A muffled, angry-sounding shout had Aspen spinning. His gaze swept the room as he readied himself to shift and fight. The sound came again, and Aspen followed it to the kitchen. His dad was tied to a chair that definitely wasn't Aspen's. Judging by the way his dad obviously couldn't break the ropes, and the way he kept barely shifting before turning human again, Aspen supposed the binds were magical in some way. He had a note pinned to his chest. *He's yours to kill. My son would never forgive me if I did away with him. How-*

ever, I **will** *be back if he isn't punished.* The signature was nothing more than some odd demonic symbol.

A loud, tired sigh came from Aspen's chest. It was always something.

Frost had no clue why he felt so much like a child waiting to be scolded for something he definitely did, as he watched Lucifer pace. Lucifer's every motion and facial expression screamed he fought for what to say. Love swelled in Frost's chest. His throat swelled. All his life, he had only had his great-aunt. Now he stared at his actual father, and so much made sense.

Lucifer stopped pacing. There was something in Lucifer's eyes. Frost moved closer to tears. An ache rolled from Lucifer. In a single glance, Frost knew he was loved and wanted. "I didn't know." Lucifer's voice sounded strained.

Riku squeezed Lucifer's shoulders. "Of course you didn't, baby. There's no way you would've left Frost out there to flounder."

Lucifer grunted.

Riku chuckled. "I know. You're still terrifying. Would it make you feel better if I added 'you're too selfish to do otherwise' to the end of that statement?"

Lucifer made another noise Frost guessed was him being mollified.

Frost's chest eased. He knew Lucifer. To his core, he didn't believe Lucifer would have abandoned him. Like Riku said, he was too selfish, but also, the first time they met, an immediate comfort had washed over Frost. Even after learning Lucifer was *the* Lucifer, Frost had felt it in his soul that Lucifer would keep him safe. Frost swallowed past his suffocating emotions. He had to remind himself feelings were amplified in Hell.

"I don't understand any of this. How did this even happen?"

Lucifer smirked at Frost's question.

Riku snorted.

Frost rolled his eyes.

Gemini snuggled his big furry leopard body even closer. He laid his head on Frost's lap.

Frost buried his fingers in Gemini's fur and massaged. He needed the comfort. "I'm being serious. Everyone let me believe my mom was some useless drug addict and my father was a random loser. I don't even know what to believe anymore."

A chair appeared, and Lucifer sat. His huge hellhound immediately moved to sit on his feet. Lucifer absently petted him. "My sister created your universe. She allowed me to play there sometimes. That's where I found a lover that

I held above all others. He was a powerful druid." He took Riku's hand and squeezed it, as if reassuring Riku he was Lucifer's one and only now. The gesture took even more weight off Frost's shoulders.

Lucifer continued. "I know you're part druid, but how much do you actually know about their world?"

Frost made a helpless gesture. "Next to nothing. No one has tried to help me learn anything about anything since I came here. There are books on druid history, but I don't know if any of those are accurate."

Lucifer nodded along, as if he suspected as much. "Don't be too hard on anyone, including yourself. Next to no one knows anything about that society. They are a hugely secretive bunch. When they die, if they actually do, their souls are reborn over and over again. They answer to no god. Magic is their master and—depending on the druid—they can be terrifyingly powerful. As you've discovered, they can cloak their entire existence and live any damn way they desire. Even the gods can't see them. But when it comes to battle, a druid is no match for a god. You might hold your own, but you can't survive one if they want you dead. And Jörmungandr wanted Bodhi dead."

"Damn. Does all this go all the way back to why you're here in the first place?"

Lucifer pulled an irritated face. "Unfortunately. As I explained, Bodhi's soul was reborn. Of course, I was here, busy creating a demon army purely from my rage. I didn't chance visiting my sister's playground again for countless years. When I did, I met another druid. As much as I hate saying this now, my only reason for seducing her was out of spite. It was proof that no one had power over me. Her aunt showed up, and I was like, 'I've got no problem with having as many beings as possible involved.' Except I immediately sensed Bodhi's soul. The recognition obviously went both ways. The woman grabbed my playmate and vanished before I snapped from my shock. I never felt the pair again. Not that I looked. By this point, Bodhi had been long forgotten. On my next visit, I felt Riku and there was no one else. I had no idea I had a son."

It hurt knowing how much of his entire life had been a lie.

"You were very well hidden from me." Lucifer sounded sad. "It took some powerful magic to hide our connection. The kind only someone like Bodhi could perform."

Frost took a steadying breath. "Well, I suppose I now know why I've been so certain you were no danger to me. From the moment we met, you've been special to me, and I didn't know why."

Riku chuckled. "I'm pretty sure everyone around you thinks you're totally mad for the way you've embraced the literal devil."

Despite everything, Frost laughed. "Yeah. I've gotten that impression a time or two."

"You're loyal." It startled Frost a little when Brownie spoke still in hellhound form. Frost hadn't known that was possible. His voice was chilling, honestly. He sounded like a beast who killed. Brownie kept going, obviously oblivious to Frost's surprise. "I smelled that on you at our first encounter. You bleed honor."

That was actually really touching. Frost didn't know what to say, especially when things turned weird.

Brownie moved to Frost and sniffed him. His nose was on Frost moving as if hunting for something.

Lucifer suddenly sat forward, looking furious. “What do you mean?” Since he directed the question toward Brownie, Frost assumed they spoke mentally.

Brownie sat. “Did you know you have a dark spell cast upon you?”

Frost blinked. “Dark spell. What?”

Brownie cocked his head to one side. “I thought you smelled different today. It’s no low-level spell. It took me a few minutes to smell it, but yep. Dark spell.” His gaze fixed on Gemini. “Has he been acting out of character?”

Gemini turned human. Thankfully, his clothes were close enough to cover his junk. He knew how jealous Frost was. Frost felt Gemini’s guilt as he responded. “He’s lost confidence in his abilities. Since he came to Wulfe, he's done so much good simply by believing in his ability to heal people. It's always been like he sees three steps ahead of everyone. Then he suddenly stopped." Gemini linked fingers with him. He didn't want to hurt Frost's feelings. Frost couldn't believe he hadn't seen all this in Gemini's mind before now. "That's the biggest reason I took him away and had my mother teach him how to cloak us. Something's wrong, but I haven't known what."

Lucifer's gaze moved over Frost. He held out his hand for Frost to take.

Frost didn't hesitate. Lucifer's eyes closed for a second. Warmth flowed from Lucifer's hand and engulfed him. It felt like being hugged from the inside.

Lucifer's eyes opened. They were a swirling mixture of black and heavenly blue. "You've been cursed by a witch. I took the poison away."

It was like a veil lifted. Until he breathed free air, he didn't realize how different his emotions were. He still had no idea what having a dark spell cast on him meant for him, but he felt better.

Lucifer didn't release his hand. He saw the way Lucifer sifted through his mind. Frost let it happen.

Lucifer smiled.

Frost had to know what he found. He turned inward and studied his mind. It didn't take long for Frost to see what Lucifer saw. Memories of his childhood flowed for Lucifer's inspection. His life flew by until he sat with his hand in Lucifer's again. *I didn't see any enemies surrounding you. But I can only see what you've seen, and you don't consider anyone a foe. They're obviously cloaked. I don't know how you were cursed, but I'll find out.* He felt Lucifer fighting for words. *Please know that you are wanted. Everything you need to thrive is already inside you. You couldn't destroy your mating if you tried. Gemini loves you. The fierceness of it coats the air. He's just scared right now. I know you're not afraid, but people will fear you. People will hunt you. You're safe in Wulfe, but outside of that town, you have to be ready to fight. Don't be afraid of your powers. Let them grow so you can protect yourself and your leopard. Know I will always come for you, because I will. You are loved, my son.*

Tears clogged Frost's throat. He had known there was a connection between them. He stared at that bond now. This was his father. Frost wanted the family he offered.

"Same."

Lucifer pulled away. His expression returned to being the cocky self Frost knew him to be. "I haven't given you a wedding gift."

A bark of laughter burst from Frost. He hugged Gemini's arm. "You don't need to give us anything. We have each other. That's the ultimate gift."

Gemini kissed his temple. *Damn straight.*

Lucifer stood. "I know everyone's deepest desires. That's my forte. Let me give you the one thing you both deeply want but never admit."

"I have no idea—"

A newborn baby appeared swaddled in his lap. "What the—"

"Your daughter. The perfect mixture of both your DNAs. You will be great parents."

For a moment, everyone seemed stunned speechless. Riku had his hand over his mouth as if even he couldn't believe what he just witnessed.

Then, Gemini reached for their daughter with shaking hands, and Frost accepted the truth. They had wished this was possible for them. More times than he could count.

Tears blurred Frost's eyes as they cuddled close and stared at their personal miracle. "She has your eyes." Frost's voice broke. "She's beautiful."

Gemini looked his way. Frost felt the love explode inside him for their family. He would be the perfect father. "Grandpa should name her, don't you think?"

They looked Lucifer's way.

Lucifer's wings were out, making him look like the god he was. Pride rolled from him. He didn't seem the least bit bothered by being called "Grandpa." "She will be Celina after her aunt. That's what I called Celeste back when we were inseparable."

Frost stared at the blessing he had been given. “Hello, Celina. We’re your dads. You have no idea how happy we are to meet you.”

Gemini kissed his temple again, and Frost saw their future. It was flawless.

Chapter Seven

A SLOW DRIP FROM the sink was the only sound in the house. Aspen sat at the kitchen table and stared at his father. Bernard had given up struggling over an hour ago. Aspen knew he thought Aspen would simply let him go soon enough. He was wrong. Aspen had no intention of being at the center of Lucifer's wrath. Unfortunately, Bernard was his father. Aspen was no killer. He had no idea what to do. His plan was to wait for Leif, but he didn't know when Leif would be home. Aspen didn't want to bother him. Frost needed to be his top priority. If Aspen called out to him, Leif would drop everything to come home. Leif showing signs of releasing his rage toward Celeste mattered to Aspen. No other god before had ever explained themselves for their actions, as far as Aspen knew. She was worthy of Leif's protection.

The smell of cotton candy filled the room. Aspen's gaze whipped toward the scent.

Celeste appeared at his side. With her gaze locked on Bernard, she squeezed Aspen's shoulder. "So this is the one who attacked my nephew." Her expression turned hard. Aspen's heart skipped a beat. He was happy not to be the focus of that look. "Pity you're not one of mine. I'd take great pleasure in reducing you to naught but dust." She cocked her head as if a sound caught her attention. A wicked smile stretched across her lips. "Luckily for me, my other half can do that."

A giant warrior with an eyepatch appeared in the room. He had to duck his head to keep from banging it on the ceiling. His wide frame took up so much space, Aspen could barely see his father. Aspen knew without asking this was Odin. Good for Celeste. He saw the appeal.

A soft, yet playful-sounding chuckle caressed his ears. He glanced Celeste's way. She stared at him with laughter in her eyes. "I know, right?"

Aspen blushed at having his thoughts read.

Odin looked over his shoulder. A wicked smile touched his lips. "Don't start. I have business with this one." His smile grew larger. "You'll have your fill later."

You are a lucky woman.

Celeste took a deep breath, as if fighting the butterflies in her stomach. "I absolutely am."

Odin's attention returned to Bernard. Aspen couldn't see his father's face, but he tensed, nonetheless. There was a crackle in the air. Odin was their god. It was his place to choose final punishment.

"You are no alpha." Total silence filled the room at Odin's words. The water didn't even drip any longer. Aspen swore he heard his father shaking.

"There's a reason you were never chosen for that position even though I know how much you coveted a leadership role. You have been given the same opportunities to thrive as every one of your Were brethren. Yet the only good thing you did was create two amazing sons, a blessing most Weres never achieve. You've already sent one home to me and sealed your fate long before today." Aspen's eyes fell closed. His chest hurt. Odin kept talking, unaware of the pain he caused.

From where Celeste's hand rested on his shoulder, a warmth spread to his chest. *He isn't unaware of your pain. There was no good way to tell you, but he can reassure you Torbren is thriving in Valhalla.*

“This is my punishment for you.”

Aspen had missed the verdict, but his father was gone. He blinked. “Is he dead?” Aspen sounded as baffled as he felt.

Odin held his stare. His electric blue eye bored into Aspen’s soul. “You are all that’s good and kind. It pains me to admit he has been sent to spend his afterlife with Lucifer. It’s a sentence unimaginably unpleasant under normal circumstances. Even I can’t imagine an eternity with Lucifer after attacking his son.”

Aspen didn’t point out he was pretty sure his dad had meant the attack for Waylon. His heart hardened a little more by the second at the knowledge his brother was gone. “Good.” He fought tears and swallowed past a swollen throat. "For Torbren's sake at the very least. He should've been put down a long time ago." The more seconds that passed, the more the truth set in. His brother was gone. Aspen supposed he had known that in his heart. There had been a reason for his panic when he had left the bubble Leif had created for them all those years ago. Since he hadn't found Torbren afterward, he had held on to a fruitless hope. He would never forgive himself for not finding a way to protect him. Now that it was too late, the knowledge he hadn't even gotten a chance to say goodbye crippled him.

The air popped and sizzled. A strong smell of alcohol overcame him. In an instant, he sat inside a vast great hall with roaring fires and unconscious men. Celeste and Odin stood at his back, holding hands.

Odin flashed a kind smile. “You have five minutes.”

Before he could process the change in scenery, someone spoke his name. “Aspen?”

Aspen’s head whipped around at his brother’s voice. “Torbren?” He looked grown and healthy. Aspen came to his feet. Torbren pulled him into a tight hug. “I can’t believe it’s you.” Aspen sniffed, trying his best to hold himself together.

Torbren pulled away, but he didn’t release Aspen’s shoulders. “Look at you. You haven’t changed at all.” His gaze slid to Aspen’s mating mark. His smile grew. "You finally got your wish. You have no idea how happy I am for you."

Aspen tried to speak through his rapid-ly swelling throat. "I can't believe you're gone. I should've stayed and protected you."

Torbren's smile turned sad. "You did all you could to keep me safe. Rest easy. There is no pain here. Food and wine flow freely. No one hurts me here."

Tears rolled down Aspen's cheeks. Tor-bren wiped them away. "None of that. I'm happy." He motioned someone for-ward, and a beautiful woman who looked like a warrior moved to stand next to him. "This is my mate, Arie. Arie, my brother, Aspen."

"It's a pleasure to meet you." Her voice was musical, and her handshake soft and warm.

"You as well." His gaze moved between the pair. This was the life he had prayed Torbren could have. Of course, Torbren had been alive in the life he envisioned. But this wasn't about him, and Aspen could live with knowing Torbren thrived, even if it was in the afterlife. "You two look perfect together."

"It's time."

At Odin's warning, Aspen tried his best to find peace. "I've decided I won't say goodbye."

Torbren smiled brightly. "Good. No one ever really dies, brother. I'm happy here."

Aspen gave him a sharp nod and took a step back. "I imagine we will be together again someday."

Torbren laughed, and Aspen sat at his kitchen table again. The chair Bernard had occupied was gone. The sound of a dripping faucet returned. Aspen was alone. He took a cleansing breath. Torbren had a good life now. Aspen was at peace with that.

No grass rustled. No twigs popped. Lysander's steps caused zero noise. He was a fairy. Lysander was in the earthly realm, but then again, he wasn't. Faerie existed all around him. The two planes were one, but they weren't. Only certain creatures and those who ate food prepared by a fairy could see the seamless union. Stone had given up on food centuries ago, and Lysander hadn't allowed Stone to drink from him. Lysander easily stalked him through the woods.

While Lysander had no idea where Stone headed, he kept pace. He needed to know what Stone had done to him. Lysander was like any other fairy. His life revolved around sex. Just as a vampire needed blood to survive, Lysander required the lust-filled energy to thrive. Sex was rarely personal with his species. Unless they found their true mate, fairies were unabashed flirts and sexual creatures. Since Lysander had allowed Stone to seduce him, something changed inside him. His thoughts were mired in jealous rage. Stone was very similar to fairy folk. He didn't hide his base needs behind a veneer of fake relationship goals. He fucked like sex was his fuel, and Lysander hadn't been right since. Lysander didn't feel this driving need to own someone the way he did with Stone. He was furious and determined. Stone would lift this spell, or Lysander would see him dead to escape this hell.

Stone stepped around a large tree and disappeared.

Lysander froze and searched his senses. It was daytime. Vampires couldn't vanish in the daylight. It was further proof of Lysander's theory. Stone wasn't—

In a breathtaking jerk, Lysander was snatched from behind and found the bark of a tree digging into his back. With an outraged vampire boxing him against the tree, Lysander couldn't see a quick escape. Truthfully, he could get away a dozen ways, but his body wouldn't obey.

"Why are you following me?" His fangs peeked out with each word, and Lysander was burning alive.

He licked his lips in his nervousness. His gaze wouldn't move from those damn fangs.

The need to feed had him in a chokehold. "You think too much of yourself. We're simply headed in the same direction."

A deadly-sounding chuckle left Stone's lips and tickled the base of Lysander's spine. "Is that so? Tell me, what place has you going my way?"

Dear King, Lysander's body begged to be touched. His throat no longer worked. He couldn't answer. Pure lust stole everything from him. As he stared into Stone's eyes, he realized the truth. Stone truly had ruined him, and now he knew why.

After an hour of searching, Audor and Leif decided their hunt was pointless. Not only was there no way they would find Frost with him being in Lucifer's clutches, but Frost was Lucifer's son. The way he deleted Bernard from existence for attacking in Frost's direction, Leif didn't believe Frost was in any danger. This wasn't the first time Lucifer had come to Frost's rescue. That didn't sound like someone bent on harming Frost. Plus, what would they realistically do anyhow? Get their legs ripped off... again. Leif had no desire to be one-legged for all eternity. Not to mention, Leif was newly mated. He only wanted to revolve around Aspen. He had something else to do first.

Leif worked as quickly as possible. He had the ability to work pretty damn fast, but making sure he achieved perfection slowed him down. An evil smile stretched his lips as he thought of Aspen's reaction. Leif didn't give Aspen a chance to guess where they were going or choose not to join him out of guilt over his father. He zapped into their home and grabbed Aspen before Aspen could say a word.

As they reappeared in the woods, Aspen held Leif's shoulders. Laughter flashed in his eyes. "Hello to you too."

Leif couldn't stop smiling. Every moment that passed in Aspen's company, the realer reality got. At first, Leif had worried he was trapped in a dream that would be ripped away from him the second his eyes opened. Somehow, no. This was all true. They had been gifted with an eternity together. He couldn't stop being floored by that truth.

"Hey, sexy bear. Did you miss me?" Without waiting for Aspen to respond, Leif skimmed Aspen's mind. His smile fell. "Why didn't you call out to me?" Now he felt like a total ass for working on a surprise while Aspen suffered alone. "I would've come straight to you. If nothing else, I could've held your hand."

Aspen kissed him. It was a sweet press of lips on lips that lingered. When he pulled away, Aspen stared at him with a love so deep, Leif got lost in its waters. Aspen held Leif's face between his hands and brushed his thumb along Leif's bottom lip. "Don't. Seriously, I'm fine. Truthfully, I'm more than fine. Torbren is thriving in a way I could only dream. Now, I don't want to ruin your surprise by reading your thoughts, so tell me. Tell me. Tell me." He hopped like a kid, bringing back the smile he loved so much. "Your excitement is too adorable. All I want is to see what has you so pleased with yourself. Give me."

Even though he still felt terrible, he believed in Aspen. Aspen wasn't.

lying. He was fine. Leif stepped back and motioned toward the hillside behind him. "It's right here."

Aspen eyed the hill, looking confused. "Okay."

Leif's smile returned. He loved making Aspen happy. He pulled open a door no one could see but him... and Aspen now. "Our love nest."

Aspen's gaze moved from the open doorway to holding Leif's stare in a snap. "Really?" His sweet bear melted. His every line screamed he was moved by the gesture.

Leif waved Aspen inside. "Go see for yourself."

Aspen twisted his fingers as he stepped through the door. "Awww. It's exactly how I pictured it."

Leif's smile grew even bigger. "I know. I can see your thoughts."

Aspen shot him a look. "Don't cheapen the moment."

Leif roared with laughter. He couldn't help it. His happiness was so huge, it had nowhere to go. Leif forced himself to stop, but the good humor could still be heard in his voice. "Yes, sir. I'll behave." A wicked smile tugged at his lips. "For now."

Aspen shook his head and focused on their surroundings. The place was no more than a pillow-covered bed, a small kitchen, and a bathroom. With a shower and tub meant for two, of course. Aspen felt the bed and opened the cabinets and fridge. After inspecting everything, he sat on the edge of the bed. Leif felt the way he had Aspen's entire focus. "You're amazing. Is this place even real, or are you straining your magic right now?"

Leif climbed onto the bed and relaxed with his fingers linked behind his head. "While I'll admit it took a huge chunk of magic to pull this off so quickly, I assure you it's real. No one can see the door to get inside, and no one can pass through the doorway except for us. This place is truly just our love cave. We can't be interrupted." Heat laced his words. "I can do anything I want to you. Anything you want."

Aspen crawled to Leif's side and cuddled close. "I want this. Me savoring every second with you while you try to seduce me the entire time." Laughter laced Aspen's words.

Leif couldn't stop smiling. "Hey. I resemble that remark." He loved the way it felt when Aspen laughed in his arms. "But you're right." He rolled so he could be the one who snuggled up in Aspen's arms. Aspen was so cuddly and gorgeous and hairy... and fuck. Leif couldn't resist him. He ran his hand up Aspen's torso, making his shirt disappear as he went. Leif buried his fingers in Aspen's chest hair before moving downward again and smoothing his hand over Aspen's sexy round stomach. There was so much of him, and he was delicious. Aspen's erection bulged in his jeans. Leif couldn't stop himself from massaging that as well.

Aspen ran Leif's long braid through his fingers. "So beautiful. I can't tell you how many nights I woke up covered in sweat and stroking myself from only dreams of you. Watching your flawless body riding my dick is seared into my brain."

Leif made the rest of Aspen's clothes vanish. He palmed Aspen's cock. His breathing quickened as he stroked Aspen. Leif could see and feel everything Aspen did.

"You've always been it for me. No one else has ever made me feel this way." Aspen sounded horny as hell.

Leif couldn't take it. In a flash, he was nude and lubed. But Leif took his time straddling Aspen's body. He held Aspen's stare as he led Aspen's dick to his asshole. "I could blow from just looking at your expression right now. You look so turned on and in love. Fuck. You have no idea how addicted I am to you. The withdrawals have been unbearable." Leif slowly took Aspen inside. He savored every huge inch, stretching him wide. He sounded as breathless as he felt when he continued. "Now that I know you're mine forever, I'm tempted to keep you this way twelve hours a day."

Something between a moan and a chuckle came from the hot beast beneath him. "Twelve hours a day, huh? We'll see." Aspen flipped. He tested every bit of Leif's flexibility as he rammed his way inside to the hilt. "You might not be able to take it. I know you like it rough, and that's how you'll get it."

Aspen didn't lie. He used every ounce of his size to control every position and thrust. There was so much dick inside him, there was no way for Aspen to miss the prostate. Leif's eyes rolled back in his head as Aspen used him like a toy. There was no mercy, and Leif loved it.

Leif flattened his hands on the headboard behind him to keep from getting fucked into the wood. Each smack of skin on skin already reverberated inside his soul. An invisible coil wound tighter inside him. Pressure built that had Leif clenching his back teeth so hard, his jaw popped. If he released a single moan or cry, Leif wouldn't know. His entire being was focused on his building orgasm. Then Aspen shoved his way inside Leif's mind, and Leif couldn't take the combined ecstasy. He turned his head and bit Aspen's forearm and drank. The force of their combined orgasm made him lose consciousness for a second. His body couldn't fathom the amount of pleasure Aspen brought him. When his mind cleared a bit, he felt the open wound on his chest healing from Aspen's bite. Leif hadn't even noticed. Everything felt too good. His mind couldn't grasp every detail.

Then Leif was snuggled in his cuddly bear's arms and savored his slice of heaven. "Goddamn, I love you."

Aspen held him tighter. "I love you too. Forever and always."

Leif would return to Celeste's service. He was man enough to admit she had seen a bigger picture of his life and kept him on the path to this endless rapture. Right now, though, Leif had no intention of leaving their new love nest. They were hidden from the world. Leif had to hang on to this peace for a while longer. The future would still be there when they emerged. For now, this was their time, and Leif didn't want to be anywhere else.

Keep an eye out for the next Devilish, *Unbewitched.*

About the Author

CHARITY PARKERSON IS AN award-winning and multi-published author with several companies. Born with no filter from her brain to her mouth, she decided to take this odd quirk and insert it in her characters. One of her greatest loves is writing morally gray characters. You'll find them scattered throughout her hundreds of titles.

*Nine-time Readers' Favorite Award Winner

*2015 Passionate Plume Award Finalist

*2013 Reviewers' Choice Award Winner

*2012 ARRA Finalist for Favorite Paranormal Romance

*Five-time winner of The Mistress of the Darkpath

Connect with her online:

*Sign up for her newsletter: https://bit.ly/charityparkersonnewsletter

*Join her readers' group on Facebook: http://bit.ly/CharitysTribe

*Website: https://www.charityparkerson.com

*A list of her social media accounts and giveaways all in one place: http://hy.page/charityparkerson

www.ingramcontent.com/pod-product-compliance
Lightning Source LLC
LaVergne TN
LVHW010653110826
845149LV00014B/3061

* 9 7 8 1 9 5 9 5 7 6 8 4 6 *